HOUSE IN THE SHADOWS

HOUSE IN THE SHADOWS

KEN RADFORD

HOLIDAY HOUSE / NEW YORK

Library of Congress Cataloging-in-Publication Data

Radford, Ken.
House in the shadows.

Summary: Emma is drawn back into time to an old inn
in a picture, where she finds a brutal man, wicked
sisters, and a starved and bullied waif who needs her
help.
[1. Space and time—Fiction]   I. Title.
PZ7.R117Ho   1987   [Fic]   87-45351
ISBN 0-8234-0673-3

Contents

CHAPTER 1

". . . with no one to watch and listen . . ."

No one knows for sure where the old boarding-house was situated. Some say it was beside a wood called Coed-y-Celyn, in the quiet countryside of North Wales. Others have heard that it stood farther to the east among the hills and scattered copses. But the old folk whose memories stretch back to the turn of the century, the time when our story begins, remember that somewhere along that winding road for horse and carriage, there stood a rambling house, hidden in the shadow of trees. Many travellers, journeying from England to Ireland, called there for supper, a mug or two of ale, and a night's rest.

"So you see, my love," old Mr Dalamore explained to his granddaughter, "there's no knowing exactly where it stood. It's so many years ago, and now there is only this faded picture to remind us of the dark deeds that went on there."

Emma peered more closely at the scene portrayed in the painting hanging in the corner of the room, at the pathway winding through the trees towards a porch hidden in the shadows, at the walls smothered with ivy, and lamplight glowing from an upstairs window.

"When you stand close and almost shut your eyes," Emma observed, "it seems so real – as if the house were standing there still, beckoning you to its doorway, as though you were a traveller of long ago."

Gently she brushed away the dust which had gathered on the canvas and wooden frame. It was strange, Emma thought, that never before had she noticed so mysterious – so sinister – a scene. But then, so many other pictures cluttered the walls of her grandfather's curiosity shop. There were ladies in crinoline dresses; gentlemen in scarlet coats riding with hounds; soldiers dying in battle; portraits of old people with stern countenances, of girls with flaxen hair and rosebud lips . . . And a hundred or more besides, resting on the floor in the corner.

"Grandad . . . " she said absently, now that the green of the trees and the silver of the moonlight shining along the path had emerged from the veil of dust which had shrouded them. "Grandad, shall we hang it near the lamp where customers can notice it? It will never catch their eyes while it's hidden in this dreary alcove."

"Tŷ-yn-y-Cysgodion – House in the Shadows – that's what it was called," her grandfather muttered, recalling memories of the past. "A house of wickedness, long since fallen down and forgotten by most. An evil place!" he went on, as though he were remembering something he would never tell. Then he shuffled off about his business, leaving Emma to continue with her dusting in the corner.

Each day she helped her grandfather in his curiosity shop, polishing and displaying his wares; and sometimes – with unusual charm for one so young – she would beguile visitors who came to browse among the shelves. "A rare treasure, sir," she would say. "A relic of the past: a keepsake to bring you good fortune . . ."

The shop stood at the cross-roads, with its windows overlooking the busy streets. Some of the panes were twisted and swirled; and when Emma peered through them at passers-by, she saw grotesque figures hurrying past, with distorted faces, or legs of remarkable length, and some with no arms at all!

The front window was arrayed with her grandfather's treasures: clocks and watches of a hundred different shapes, ticking away from morning till night. Behind them stood the stately clocks whose pendulums, swaying from side to side, sometimes caught the glint of the evening sun. Whenever Emma lingered a while, listening to them, she felt that time was rushing by, paying little heed to a fair-haired girl who spent her days pottering only among memories of long ago.

There was little room to roam around among the brass lamps and pewter jugs, the bronze plaques and chinaware, and a thousand curios which lay on the shelves. While her grandfather was mending clocks in the back room, and her grandmother was busy upstairs in the kitchen, Emma was seldom lonely, for there were always the people in the pictures, looking down from their frames with a smile or a frown. They were always there to keep her company. And although she rarely escaped the confines of the curiosity shop, she could, in her imagination, journey to the far-away places portrayed in the scenes hanging all about her: to the wild moors of Yorkshire, the lochs and braes of the Highlands, the emerald hills of Ireland; even across the oceans to cities far off to the east and west.

Yet, of all the paintings of distant lands and cities and moon-lit shores, none captured her interest nor stirred her imagination more than Tŷ-yn-y-Cysgodion, with its mouldering roof, walls clad with ivy, and lamplight glowing in an attic window.

"Grandad," Emma called without turning around, "long

9

ago, before the tavern was deserted – before its walls crumbled away – who lived there?"

She had taken the picture from the corner of the room and had hung it where the light of the lamp fell upon it. Now she stood gazing along the path which wound through the trees towards the porch.

The old man was behind the counter, reckoning the day's takings and putting the coins into a tin box.

"Two old crones, I've heard tell," he replied. "Sisters, they were, with faces all wrinkled and backs crooked with age. Dead and gone now, and the travellers thereabouts well rid of them, I shouldn't wonder."

"Who would wish to shelter in a creepy old house, hidden among the trees?" Emma wondered.

"Travellers, journeying by coach from England to Ireland, and overtaken by nightfall, and likely, farmers of the parish thirsting after a long day in the fields. But as the years wore on, and stories were told, no one dared spend the night there."

"No one?"

"Just the two old harridans," her grandfather said, "roaming the dark rooms and corridors, hatching some mischief or other."

Emma's eyes sparkled with interest. "Witches, perhaps, muttering spells to lure travellers back again!"

The old man dropped a coin on the floor, and searched for it among the assortment of vases and furniture strewn upon the boards.

"Were they, Grandad?" Emma urged. "Were they really witches, with tall hats and knobbly sticks and shawls wrapped about their shoulders?"

The old man's thoughts returned to mundane matters. He abandoned his search, straightening his back with a sigh. "Come along, my love. It's time for supper. Help me fasten the shutters and draw down the blinds. It's been a long day."

Presently the door was bolted, and the snowflakes that swirled about the window could no longer be seen. Before they turned down the lanterns that lit the shop, Emma's eyes lingered on the picture, now hanging in its new position.

"I wonder who could be up there, all alone perhaps, in the lamplight of an attic room?"

Then together they climbed the stairs where, in the living rooms above the shop, Emma's grandmother was preparing their supper.

A fire was blazing in the grate. On the hob beside it, a cauldron of stew was bubbling, and the smell of new-baked bread wafted from the oven. Three places were set at the table, and dishes were laid upon the fender to warm.

As they sat down to their evening meal, Emma's thoughts still dwelt on the painting she had discovered beneath a veil of dust.

"Gran," she ventured, touching her hand to hold her attention, "do you remember an old tavern which once stood by the woods at Coed-y-Celyn?"

Her grandmother pondered for a moment and then said: "I've heard of such a place; but that was many years ago. It's long since fallen to ruin and been forgotten. Besides, no God-fearing folk would ever cross the threshold!"

"An evil place!" her grandfather reflected, "if all the stories told are true."

"House in the Shadows . . ." Emma murmured to herself, wondering whether it was the shadows of the surrounding trees or shadows of evil that had given the house its name. And then, remembering how the porch was

11

plunged in darkness, and the solitary light glowing in the window of an upstairs room, she said to her grandparents: "Perhaps the house was haunted!"

She paused for a while, lost in thought. "I wonder if sometimes," she went on, "sometimes, when the moon is bright and all around is quiet, with not a soul about to watch and listen . . . I wonder if Tŷ-yn-y-Cysgodion appears there at the edge of the woods, as large as life – just as it used to be all those years ago. Maybe – with no one there to see – horse-drawn carriages go trundling along the pathway through the trees; and the windows are all aglow with lights; and the sound of folk laughing and singing comes drifting out; and at the doorway two old women appear . . ."

"Good heavens, child!" her grandmother interrupted. "Your imagination is blazing away like wildfire! Whatever will you be dreaming of next!"

"It could be so," Emma insisted, "when there's not a living soul about to watch and listen."

After supper they sat around the fire while, outside, the driven snow nestled on the window ledge and muffled the steps of passers-by. With her sewing basket beside her, Nell Dalamore was busy with her needle and thread, listening with some misgiving as the old man grumbled of hard times and of declining business through the winter months.

"All day long, folk hurry past with never a glance in the window," he complained.

"Don't fret so," his wife comforted. "When winter has gone, and the weather is fine again, visitors will come to town with money to spend and souvenirs to take away."

After a while Emma tired of her storybooks for, in the evenings when the shutters had been fastened against the windows of the curiosity shop and she and her grandfather had gone to the upstairs rooms, she had read them over and over again. Now she drew back the curtains and looked down upon the streets all edged with drifts of snow; and at the lamplighter trudging along with his long pole, leaving pools of gold upon the pavement and flurries of white to dance in the glow of gas-light. Roof-tops and chimneys stood dark against the sky.

"If I were to wrap up warm," she wondered, "and wander far off towards the woods at Coed-y-Celyn, where there is no other soul for miles around . . . Would I come upon a pathway winding through the trees? And if I dared go farther, would a lonely house appear – Tŷ-yn-y-Cysgodion – in the place it stood all those years ago?"

Emma's imagination smouldered on. She had travelled no distance from home during the thirteen years of her childhood, not since that day, too long ago for her to remember, when as a young orphan she had come to live with her grandparents. Yet, in her thoughts and dreams her journeying knew no bounds.

"What if I were to unfurl that Persian carpet – one of Grandad's valuable antiques – rolled up in the corner beneath the stairs? If I were to whisper a magic spell? Then, surely, it would float through the air, rising high above the roof-tops. It would carry me across the seas to a far-off land, like a princess in a fairy story.

"Over hills and deserts I would drift, passing high above the pyramids of Egypt and the temples of Siam, farther even than all the places shown in the pictures hanging on the walls downstairs . . ."

The evening wore on. Presently her grandfather called from the fireside, disturbing Emma's voyage of make-believe. "Come along, my Beautiful Dreamer," he said, remembering the title of an old song. "Tomorrow is another long day."

Emma's bedroom was near the top of the stairs. If all were quiet, and she raised her head from the pillow, she could hear the clocks ticking away the hours of darkness, and chiming as each one passed. Hurried ticking and slower, measured beats, like the footsteps of children and grown-up folk walking together along the cobble-stones in the street. Then a confusion of sounds as solemn chimes and cuckoo calls spelled out that night was stealing by.

Emma slept fitfully, her thoughts and dreams flitting from a rambling house hidden in the shadows to journeying over exotic lands on a magic carpet.

By and by an unusual sound prompted her to sit up in bed and listen. From somewhere below the stairs there came a wailing, like the sound of wind under the eaves. She lit the candle and looked around her room. The curtains at the window did not stir. She opened the door and listened at the top of the stairs.

Standing there on the landing, with the shadows of the banister rails flickering upon the wall, Emma became afraid; for now the rushing and moaning of the wind grew louder.

There was a tremble in her voice as she whispered to herself: "It's not the sound of the wind outside! It's here inside the house! It's coming from somewhere down there! From the darkness of Grandad's curiosity shop!"

CHAPTER 2

". . . somewhere in the darkness below the stairs . . ."

It was some time before the sound of the wind went away, and the curiosity shop below the stairs was quiet again. Emma returned to her room and looked out through the window. Snowflakes were no longer swirling about the street lamps, but now gathered in drifts against the walls and in sheltered corners, glistening in the gas-light, while above the roof-tops the sky was sprinkled with stars. This way and that she looked along the deserted street, but there was not a soul to be seen. At length she climbed back into her bed, held the clothes close to her chin, and lay there listening . . . wondering. Then, from downstairs, came the chimes and cuckoo calls to announce the hour of midnight.

It was still dark outside when she awakened next morning. By the time she had washed and put on her clothes, the fire was ablaze and the kettle was singing on the hob. She looked forward to when her lessons were over, so that she could hurry home to begin another evening of dusting and polishing, or smiling at anyone who chanced to wander into the shop and browse among the curios on display.

"Last night . . ." she began, when they were sitting down to their breakfast, "not long after I had fallen asleep, I heard the wind howling; but when I looked out from the window, the sky was clear and the street was all calm – with not a breath of wind to stir the curtains."

"It's the clear sky in winter that brings the frost," her grandfather complained. "Few folk will venture out of doors on such a chilly morning."

"Strange that everything should be so still," Emma continued absently, "when the wind is howling so. Not outside – but somewhere in the darkness below the stairs . . ."

"It must have been the chiming of the clocks that woke you." Her grandmother's brow furrowed as she looked at Emma with some concern. "If your rest is broken night after night, dark shadows will appear under your eyes."

But Emma was once more lost in thought. "Sighing and wailing . . . far away and yet so near . . . somewhere down in the darkness . . ." she went on muttering to herself.

Resigned, her grandmother left Emma to her day-dreams. "Heavens child," she sighed, gathering the dishes from the table, "there's nothing downstairs but your grandfather's clocks and ornaments; and a jumble of old furniture down in the cellar."

Many times that winter, about the hour the clocks struck twelve, the same sound came back to haunt Emma. Each time her nightmare – if indeed it was a nightmare – became more vivid. Sometimes she ventured half-way down the stairs and let the candle-light chase the shadows around the walls. But there her courage always failed, and she hurriedly retraced her steps to listen from the landing. Then, when morning came her fears faded, when the clocks and curios and ornaments of china and brass and pictures hanging all about were found resting unharmed in their accustomed places. Not even a picture was crooked.

Once, when she woke, she knocked on the door of her grandparents' bedroom and cried out: "Grandad, come quickly! It's back again – the wind whistling and howling! Come quickly!"

However, no sooner had her grandfather appeared in the doorway than the sound went away, leaving the house in silence again.

"What is it?" he said sleepily.

Emma pointed to the darkness below the stairs. "There's the sound of a fierce wind . . . like a storm approaching! And this time the darkness was lit with flashes of light . . . and I heard the rumble of thunder!"

Then she saw the face of her grandmother, looking over the old man's shoulder, with startled eyes.

He took the candle from Emma and led the way along the landing and down the stairs. The curiosity shop was wrapped in darkness, and now there was no sound to disturb the silence. Her grandparents tried as best they could to dispel her fears.

"You see, there's no one – not a sound. There are only the clocks ticking away through the night, and counting out the hours . . ."

"Heavens, child, it's just a dream tormenting you. Soon it will go away and trouble you no more."

And for a while Emma's recurring nightmare did go away. Each day passed as uneventfully as the last, with her grandfather sitting at his bench tending his clocks, her grandmother moving around in the rooms overhead, going about all her household tasks. And Emma . . . well, her thoughts were seldom free of romantic notions and visions of far away and long ago, all conjured up in her imagination.

Then there came an evening close to Christmas, when

17

the curiosity shop remained open later than usual, for now folk had come to peer into the window or search among the shelves for rare gifts to buy for their loved ones. It had been a busy day, but old Mr Dalamore was well content, for his tin box was heavy with coins.

It was past supper time before people began to leave the streets and make their way home. The shutters had been fastened, and Emma's grandfather was already climbing the stairs, while Emma was turning down the lights. One by one the lamps were extinguished, plunging each corner into darkness, until the only lamp burning cast its light on the picture of Tŷ-yn-y-Cysgodion. Although she was weary after a long day, she could not resist a moment's glance at the path through the trees and its ivy shroud all bathed in moonlight, and . . . Startled, she looked again, her eyes fixed on the sky. Her heart leapt when, for an instant, she fancied that the scene became darker as a cloud passed over the face of the moon. Strange how the lamplight played tricks with her imagination, she thought.

Emma moved closer, staring up at the likeness of the old house. But no . . . it was not an illusion. She backed away in disbelief. Clouds were hurrying across the sky, throwing swathes of light and shadow upon the building and the trees surrounding it. Farther away along the horizon were flashes heralding the approach of a storm; and boughs which overhung the pathway were swaying from side to side.

At first the sound of the wind was only a whisper; then it grew in volume to a sorrowful sigh, although she felt no breath of it. And from somewhere – far-off it seemed, and for no longer than a moment or two – came the swell of voices, though whether shouting or singing in discord it was difficult to tell.

Emma's cries of astonishment brought her grandfather in haste back down the stairs to see what had startled her.

"The picture – it's come to life!" she exclaimed. "The clouds and trees are moving in the wind!"

"Emma . . . Emma . . . it's just an old painting; just the light of the lamp flickering . . ."

"But I saw the boughs brushing against the sky, and heard voices coming from the tavern!"

The old man looked into the picture; but there was no sign of movement within the frame, nor even a whisper from the scene portrayed there. He turned out the lamp hanging from the ceiling, placed his hand gently on Emma's shoulder, and led her to the stairs. "Come along, my dreamer," he smiled. "With your imagination some day you will become the finest storyteller in all Wales."

"It was not a dream!" Emma protested, tears of frustration welling up in her eyes. "The noise of the wind and thunder that woke me in the night . . . lightning flashing in the sky . . . the sound of voices calling . . . It was all so real! They come from the tavern at Coed-y-Celyn. Why does no one believe me?"

However hard he tried to understand the strange notions which upset her so, her grandfather could not help but chuckle to himself at such a peculiar story.

They ate their supper in silence that evening, for Emma's grandmother would listen to no more tales of storms and ghostly voices emanating from the picture of Tŷ-yn-y-Cysgodion which hung on the wall of the curiosity shop. "Come morning," she said, "your grandfather will put it back in the cellar, for that's where it's been lying all these years, gathering dust and cobwebs. Then there'll be no sounds to wake you from your sleep!"

For a long time that night Emma lay in her bed, listening

and wondering; but no sighing wind or distant peals of thunder came from below the stairs.

It was Saturday. The morning was cold, with clear skies allowing the sun to filter between the buildings and melt away patches of snow which lay along the street. When her dusting and polishing were done, Emma whiled away the time peering through the spiral panes of glass, and chuckling with amusement at the strange proportions of the men and women who passed by the window.

"Isn't it amusing, grandad," she laughed. "It's just like the hall of mirrors at the fun-fair!"

The old man was standing on a chair, taking down the picture which he had promised to return to the cellar.

Emma left the window and came to stand beside him. It was such an intriguing picture; and although at times it had frightened her – yet it still fascinated her. It was just as one dreads the sheer face of a precipice, but is still drawn nearer its edge. In the dark and dust of the cellar it would lie forgotten – perhaps for always.

Thoughts whirled through her mind. "One night, when all is quiet, I will steal down the stairs and rescue it from the cellar . . . keep it hidden in my room . . ." But she knew that it would be discovered, that her grandmother would frown on her mischief. "Maybe I could sell it to some wealthy customer who comes searching for an unusual work of art? . . ." But who would buy the painting of a shadowy house? Perhaps she could invent some romantic story: some legend which would throw a different complexion on the tale of Tŷ-yn-y-Cysgodion?

Emma's eyes sparkled. "Yes . . . that's what I shall do. I shall use my imagination, and change its wicked past!" After all, she reasoned, if she happened to be alone with a customer in the shop no one need ever know.

"Please!" she said, pulling at her grandfather's sleeve, "leave it for a few more days – just until Christmas has gone. Someone is sure to admire it."

Her grandfather relented, for whenever Emma's deep blue eyes met his he could never refuse her wishes. "Just until Christmas has gone," he agreed, "if you promise there'll be no more fairy tales of storms raging in the night, and trees and clouds moving in the wind."

Emma gave no such promise. Even now, as her eyes searched through the shadows under the porch and the mantle of green that clung to the walls, she fancied that the light burning in the attic window was flickering.

On Christmas Eve Emma decorated the walls with bright trimmings, and the shop window was strewn with tinsel which sparkled in the light. Outside, a band of street musicians had gathered under the lamp at the corner, to play carols and accept coppers from those who were kind enough to give them. A flow of people passed by, muffled up against the chill of winter, their baskets laden with presents and Christmas fare. Some pressed their faces against the window to scan the assortment of clocks and pocket-watches and curios displayed there. Time and again, Emma wound the clockwork music boxes arrayed on the shelves, so that when the bell above the door tinkled and someone came inside, there was a blend of soft lights, with a medley of ticks and chimes and cuckoo calls and melodies played in dulcimer tones – all designed to tempt their curiosity.

It was later that Christmas Eve, almost time for them to fasten the shutters and turn down the lights, when a gentleman wearing a tall hat and fine overcoat entered the shop. He wandered around among the shelves, raising the lid of each music box in turn and listening to the tune it played. Then he looked about, examining the plates and pictures which hung upon the walls.

Old Mr Dalamore was in the back room repairing his clocks. Looking over her shoulder, Emma could see him bending low over his work-bench, engrossed in some delicate task and oblivious of all else around him. Her heart was beating as fast as the clocks and a mischievous twinkle danced in her eyes, for the stranger who had come to look around wore the clothes and bearing of one blessed with wealth and position.

"Most things you see are very old," she ventured. Then, with softened voice and a hint of nostalgia: "Once they were someone's treasures – all memories of long ago. Perhaps there is something special you wish to see?"

"There are so many things to choose from," the man frowned as he continued to search the walls. "I'm looking for a present for my daughter, a gift she could cherish. She's not strong enough to run around as most children do, and presents bring her such pleasure."

Emma began to tingle with excitement. The stranger looked at her and pondered for a while, perhaps wondering whether he should ask to see the proprietor. "She's a girl no older than you – and almost as pretty," he smiled.

"My grandfather says I am as old as Methuselah!" Emma laughed to hide her embarrassment.

"Well, young lady – I wonder . . . if I should ask, which from all these treasures would you choose for yourself? Then I should know what my daughter might like."

Emma looked about her: at the delicately fashioned brooches and pendants, charm stones and cuckoo clocks, jewel boxes lined with velvet which played sad lullabies . . . Then her eyes strayed to the wall. "A painting, perhaps?"

she suggested. "A picture to hang beside her bed: a scene to gaze into and wonder, and wish that she were there. If someone were to ask, that's what I would choose."

The man moved closer to the wall, standing with the lamp behind him, studying the portraits and landscapes. Emma's choice seemed to appeal to him. "Something to stir the imagination, and brighten her spirits," he mused. "A picture of a foreign land, perhaps – far across the sea?" the gentleman muttered to himself. "Somewhere she might never travel except in her imagination . . ."

He noticed that Emma's eyes were fixed on the picture of the House in the Shadows, stark in the moonlight. He could never have guessed what memories were passing through her thoughts.

"A scene of mystery," he muttered thoughtfully, viewing the picture with interest. "Is this the one you would choose?"

He fancied he could see tears misting Emma's eyes when she began her story.

"There's a strange tale told about the house in this picture," she said quietly. "My grandfather first heard it long ago. They say that once it was the home of two kindly old ladies, with little wealth, but hearts of gold . . ." She glanced slyly towards the stranger; but his eyes were on the picture. "Whenever folk were hungry and homeless, the old ladies gave them food and shelter, asking nothing in return.

"My grandmother says that the house has long since fallen to ruin, and its walls have all crumbled away. Even all those years ago it was old and barely furnished. But there was always a blazing fire in the hearth on winter nights, and a warm welcome at the threshold for poor souls who had lost their way. *The Travellers' Rest,* it was called. Perhaps you have heard the story before?"

The gentleman shook his head solemnly, and Emma was encouraged to continue with her story.

"The story goes that although the ladies were old and frail, the Fair Folk – fairies from the Otherworld – looked over them, guarding them from sickness and danger. The fire was always banked high with peat and the larder replenished with bread and cheese and jars of honey; yet no one knows by what magic the fuel and food appeared there.

"And once there came a robber, sneaking in after dark. He was seen running off to the woods, with his eyes wide with terror and his hands all charred and withered away!

"After nightfall, so the story goes, when everyone was in bed, the Fair Folk would come from the dells to scrub and bake and weave their magic spells. Then when their toil was over they gathered together in an attic room to play their fairy music in the lamplight, so that every weary traveller would be lulled into a deep sleep and wake bright and fresh in the morning."

Emma paused to point into the picture. "See how all the house is dark while a lamp burns in the attic window."

She heard her grandfather shuffling around in the back room, and knew that his day's work was almost done.

"That was all a long time ago," she went on, "and perhaps only a story which was never true. The house has gone now, and the old ladies long since dead and buried. But they say that where they lie, the grass is always fresh and green, and sweet-smelling flowers grow about their graves: rare and beautiful they are, blooming all summer and winter too."

"Then if someone were to ask what gift you liked best, would you choose this picture of *The Travellers' Rest*?" the gentleman asked.

"My grandfather always says it's the finest painting we have, and specially valuable because, save for the stories the old folk remember, there is only the picture to remind us that the house was ever there."

The customer put his cane upon the counter and fumbled in his purse. "Perhaps you could persuade your grandfather to part with it," he said. Then into Emma's hand he pressed a generous number of golden coins.

CHAPTER 3

". . . another place – another time . . ."

Emma felt sad to see the man leaving the shop with the picture tucked under his arm. Perhaps it was because she would no longer have a spark to set her imagination alight, and could now never unfold the mystery of clouds moving across the sky, or the sighing of the wind which often had awakened her.

It was not until the gentleman had closed the door behind him that she showed her grandfather the golden coins glistening in her hand.

"That old picture – the House in the Shadows –" she said, "it's gone. While you were busy in the back room, a rich gentleman came to admire it, and buy it for his daughter as a Christmas gift."

She was afraid to tell of her account of the saintly ladies and the Fair Folk who watched over them, for fear of incurring her grandfather's displeasure. In this time of hardship, they gleaned only a meagre living from the clocks and curios they sold; but the old man was always honest and fair in his dealings.

Astonished, he gazed at the coins, unable to believe his eyes. "It's a small fortune – much more than the picture was worth!" Uneasily, he paced back and forth, wondering what best to do. Then he stood in the doorway and looked along the street. But there was no sign of the gentleman with the tall hat and fine overcoat. "It's likely he's made a mistake," Mr Dalamore decided. "Make haste, child; you must find him! He can't have gone far."

Anxiously, Emma hurried off in the direction the man had taken, past the shops and rows of tenements, to the farthest end of the street. But he was nowhere in sight.

It was not just the bitter wind that brought tears to her eyes. She had imagined that the reward she had reaped from her storytelling would have brought pleasure to her grandfather, instead of upsetting him so. How many times had she worried and wondered when folk passed by the curiosity shop, never sparing a minute to come inside. All day long the old man worked hard, tinkering with his clocks and watches; yet there was little to show for his pains. It made Emma sad to see no sparkle in his eyes – no smile on his face.

"After all," she muttered to herself, "the picture had some mystery – some magic – about it." Besides, had the man not chosen it himself – persuaded perhaps by her fanciful story? Was it mischievous, she wondered, to make up such tales? "Anyway," she argued with her conscience, "from his fine clothes and easy bearing it was clear to see that he was a wealthy gentleman, and could well afford the money he paid."

And so Emma wrestled with her thoughts as she searched in vain among the people in the street for the man who was carrying away the picture of Tŷ-yn-y-Cysgodion. At length she made her way home, her head hung low, for her endeavour to brighten the old man's spirits had gone awry.

"Some day he'll come along," her grandparents said. "We shall keep his money safe until he visits us again."

27

The following day the incident was not mentioned, and the shutters on the window of the curiosity shop remained fastened. Patches of snow still lay on the roof-tops and in the streets, sparkling in the pale rays of the sun. They were making their way home from church, and Emma was reflecting now, not on the generosity of the gentleman to whom she had sold the picture, but on the deeds of a kindly king who trudged through the cruel wind, bearing food and pine logs to a poor soul with little to fend off the cold of winter; not of moonlight shining upon a house in the shadows, but of a bright star appearing in the sky, and of shepherds gazing at it in wonder.

"Grandad," she said as they strolled along, "at school we learned of a bright light moving across the heavens, coming to rest and shining down upon the stable where Jesus was born. Would that star appear to everyone, or only to those who believed that something mysterious – something wonderful – was happening? Do folk sometimes see things that are hidden from others?"

"Only when they drift off into dreams, or a spark sets alight their imagination," her grandfather answered with a mischievous smile.

Emma smiled back at him, and for the remainder of their journey home she sang quietly to herself the words of Christmas carols she could remember.

Their day was spent peacefully, for they were content to remain indoors, thankful for the comfort of their fireside. There was the sizzling and spluttering of roast goose in the oven. Humble gifts were given one to another and they played music on a phonograph which had lain unwanted among the relics on a shelf downstairs.

"Wouldn't it be wonderful," Emma sighed as she wished her grandparents good-night, "if all the year long everyone was as kindly as at Christmas time?"

Days passed by; and although Emma was ever watchful when the bell above the shop door tinkled and when distinguished gentlemen walked past the window, the stranger who came on Christmas Eve did not call again.

Then, one morning early in the new year, a young woman wearing a cloak and bonnet entered the shop. She stood at the counter, looking about her with some anxiety. Under her arm she carried a picture with a length of cloth wound around it.

"Begging your pardon, sir," she said to Mr Dalamore. "My master has sent me along with this picture, and a message for the young miss — the fair girl with the blue eyes, he says."

"Ah . . . yes . . . there's been some misunderstanding," the old man faltered. "We were hoping he would call again." He hastened up the stairs to fetch the golden coins which had been put away for safe-keeping, leaving Emma with the visitor to offer some explanation.

"You're the one right enough, miss," the maid-servant observed, peering into Emma's face. "I can tell from my master's description. Christmas Eve it was, you remember — late in the evening?"

Emma unwrapped the cloth cover and looked once more upon the shadowy house portrayed there in the moonlight. "The gentleman came to search for a gift to give his daughter," she recalled. "For a long time he looked around, but nothing else took his fancy. He seemed well pleased with the picture," Emma went on defensively, "and paid much more than it was worth, although I did not know the true value of the picture then. Perhaps I should have . . ."

"A kindly gentleman, that he is," the messenger

interrupted. "I am to tell you, miss, that he wishes you to have the picture, for he remembers how you spoke of it with deep feeling that brought tears to your eyes. He was very taken with you, miss. More than likely it's because you remind him so of his own daughter. 'Give it to the young lady with fair hair and blue eyes,' that's the instructions he gave me. 'Tell her that the old *Travellers' Rest* is now hers to enjoy.'"

"But . . . his daughter?" Emma said. "He bought the picture as a gift for her."

The servant looked over her shoulder when she heard the old man coming down the stairs. She lowered her voice. "She didn't take kindly to the old house in the picture, miss. If the truth be told, it frightened her. There it was hanging in her bedroom, with the light of the lamp shining on it; and never a night passed that she didn't wake with bad dreams, and cried out for her mother and father. Dark shadows under her eyes, she had – and in the end too afraid to go alone to her bed." Now her eyes were opened wide. "You would never believe," she continued in a whisper, "that once she fancied the wind was howling through the shutters of that old house, and voices were calling from inside. Funny how children's imaginations run wild when nightfall comes. Then she heard . . ."

Her voice trailed away as the old man approached with his hand outstretched. "Give this to your master," he said with a smile. "Tell him I'm sorry for the misunderstanding. Perhaps some day he will call again to look around . . ."

"No, sir! Thank you all the same." The young woman retreated towards the door, her hands held behind her back. "I mustn't take a penny. The picture was sold in good faith, my master says; and now the young girl must have it for her own, to do with as she pleases, for she always liked it so – that's what he says. Good day, sir, and thank you." She turned to Emma. "And my master hopes it brings you pleasure, miss."

So saying, the woman opened the door, and with a slight curtsey, hurried off past the window and out of sight, leaving the old man to gaze upon the golden coins he held in his hand.

"Bless my soul!" Emma's grandmother gasped, when she had listened to the story. "Then now the old picture is yours, my love," she said to her granddaughter. "But not to stare into and imagine ghostly sounds of Tŷ-yn-y-Cysgodion coming back from the past – and then haunt you in your dreams!" she scolded.

Mr Dalamore jingled the coins in his jacket pocket. "And there will be stout shoes and a warm overcoat for you to wear to school when the holidays are over."

"And a new dress and bonnet, and a Sunday suit, for an elegant Gran and Grandad to wear to church," Emma laughed.

"And a tidy sum left over to put away for a rainy day," the old man reckoned.

It warmed Emma's heart to see the smile on her grandfather's face, and the twinkle in his eyes.

As for the shadowy house, bathed in moonlight and mystery – that was restored to its position on the wall, where, in the long evenings of winter, the glow of the lamp fell upon it. And there it remained, through daylight and lamp-shine and dark, with never a sound nor movement to distinguish it from the other pictures hanging there. Although now it belonged to her, Emma was a little afraid to hang it in her room where it would be close to her while she slept.

With the spring term now wearing on, and school friends

to keep her company, Emma's thoughts dwelt on other things; and she spent little time helping her grandfather in the curiosity shop. Only occasionally did she look at the picture of Tŷ-yn-y-Cysgodion; and when she did, there seemed nothing peculiar in its appearance to hold her attention. Not until one night at the end of the winter.

Emma was awakened by the same sound she had heard on previous occasions: a sighing and whistling as low as the cry of an owl – as when the March winds rush under the eaves. It blew continuously; and the longer she listened the more furious it became.

As she raised her head from the pillow, the chiming of the clocks downstairs sounded the hour of midnight. The last chimes had died away when she threw aside the bedclothes. After a while, she dared to hold the door ajar. The ghostly wind howled louder still, but it did not hurl clocks and ornaments from their resting place, nor come rushing up over the stairs to blow out her candle. As had happened before, she felt not even a breath of it.

Afraid to venture farther, Emma closed the door and laid down the candle. Then for a long time she buried her head under the bedclothes, waiting for the sound to go away.

The following night it came again – not this time at midnight, when the house was in darkness and everyone was asleep, but while Emma was alone downstairs, putting out the lamps one by one.

The clocks had just struck eight when she became aware of movement on the wall, and a rustling close by. Looking up, she saw that it was not something she had imagined – not a flickering of the lamp. The boughs overhanging the pathway which led to the house in the picture were swaying from side to side. And there was no mistaking the plaintive sigh of the wind or the changing pattern of the clouds as they passed over the face of the moon; for there were moments when the walls and roof were hidden in darkness, and Emma could see only the light shining from the attic window.

Fascinated, she could neither cry out nor turn her eyes away. It was as though she were held spellbound. As she gazed into the picture, she was astonished at its transformation. Taking on a mysterious dimension, the sky expanded over and around her; and in the depths of it the horizon was lit up by intermittent flashes. The house grew to real proportions as she moved along the pathway and caught glimpses of it through the trees that passed her by. She felt the touch of overhanging boughs and the wind ruffling her hair. There was no chill of winter in the air, but more the softness of a summer night.

Emma looked back over her shoulder. There was no lamp-light throwing shadows upon the walls and among the clocks of the curiosity shop. There was only a path stretching behind her. Some awesome spell had spirited her away to a place and a time she had known only in her imagination. Now the ivy-clad walls and shadowy porch of Tŷ-yn-y-Cysgodion stood there before her – not fifty steps away.

CHAPTER 4

". . . You are a ghost, aren't you? . . ."

The distant flashes drew nearer, streaking across the sky, and for moments changing the dark to daylight. The moon was now hidden behind black clouds which moved swiftly overhead. Emma jumped with fright at a sudden crack of thunder. Then rain began to fall: heavy drops at first, and intermittently, like foot-falls all around her. But it soon became a deluge, lashing upon the trees and path until her dress clung to her legs and shoulders and her hair fell limp before her eyes.

The silhouette of the house merged with the darkness, with only the light in the attic window to show it was still there. Emma dared not shelter beneath the trees, so she stumbled forward until she reached the awning above the porch.

Perhaps it had been the rage of the storm that drowned the sound of voices from within the tavern, for standing there near the doorway she now heard laughter and raucous singing. The shutters were closed, with no light escaping through the windows, but clearly the lower rooms were not deserted, as at first she had imagined.

Emma waited under the porch, all the while listening and wondering, until the thunder rolled by, and the moon reappeared from behind the clouds. Presently there was a swell of voices from inside the tavern as the door was opened and two men, roughly clad in the clothes of countrymen, came out into the moonlight. They came upon her so suddenly that she was too surprised to steal out of sight.

"I . . . I was caught in the storm . . . There was nowhere else to shelter," she stammered.

Leaving the door open, the men came forward, paying no heed to the girl who stood in their path. Close they came, and closer still, until they were almost upon her.

"I'm sorry," said Emma, backing away. "I thought no one lived here. You see . . ." she went on, not knowing quite how to explain her presence there, "you see, I've lost my way. I come from . . ." She wondered whether it would be true to say "far away", but she said no more. Instead she let out a startled cry and looked about her in astonishment, for they neither paused to listen, nor even made any effort to step aside. They walked straight ahead – passed right through her, as though she were not there at all! Emma could only turn and stare as they made off along the path.

After a while, the singing inside the tavern ceased; but the hubbub of voices continued, although none was clearly audible. She approached the doorway and peered in. The room was dimly lit by lamps which hung from stout beams across the ceiling, and around which swirled halos of smoke. Crudely fashioned tables, strewn with mugs, filled the alcoves and stood against the walls. And around them people were gathered in groups: young men and old; gentlemen and farm workers; and here and there were women with painted lips, their voices shrill above the others. All were engaged in noisy conversation and merriment. Casks of ale lay on a counter, tended by a sturdy man with a scarred face – likely a relic of some dark deed, Emma imagined. In the lamp-light and from a distance he had about him the look of someone with a cruel heart.

Evan Du – Black Evan – he was called, for once in a while Emma heard folk shout out his name whenever their mugs were to be replenished. With a shiver, she wondered whether it was the dark clothes he wore or his black heart that earned him such a name.

For a long time she stood at the door, watching their mirth, listening to the laughter and occasional song. But no one seemed to notice her standing there. Even when men passed through the doorway, close enough for her to reach out and touch them, not one so much as glanced her way.

"If some spell has drawn me here," Emma murmured to herself, "backwards in time, to a place which is only a memory – then to those who lived in this Otherworld I must be just a ghost, for I am not really here at all!" Now she could wander at will among them – unnoticed, safe from any peril.

"Hullo!" she called from the doorway, and then again, louder – above the noise issuing from inside. "Hullo! Can you hear me?"

But no one paid the slightest attention to her calling. After all, Emma reasoned, in this present time, were they not all dead and gone, existing only in her imagination?

Bolder now, she crossed the threshold and went inside the tavern, passing so close to Evan Du that she felt as though his cold eyes were looking directly into hers, and that at any moment he would stretch out his hand and seize her.

In the far corner there were stairs leading up into the darkness; and a voice somewhere in Emma's thoughts

began to whisper: "If I were to climb the stairs, and close
my eyes, and drive away all images of this place, then
perhaps I shall find myself back on the stairs in the corner
of the curiosity shop; and the clocks will have just struck
eight; and Gran's voice will be calling me to supper . . ."

So she hurried past the burning eyes of Evan Du and the
folk gathered around the casks of ale, until she reached the
foot of the stairway. There she closed her eyes tightly; and
with all the concentration she could muster, imagined that
she could hear the ticking of her grandfather's clocks – that
he and her grandmother would be there to greet her on the
landing.

Step by step she ascended, hoping and wishing all the
while. Then a frightening realisation made her heart leap.
If this spell were to remain, there was no telling when she
would find her way back to the time where she belonged.
Perhaps she was doomed to stay forever among the people
of years gone by!

Climbing up into the darkness, Emma heard the voices in
the tavern grow faint, but they did not die away; nor did
she find herself in a place with which she was familiar. A
shaft of moonlight came slanting in through a window at
the end of the corridor upstairs, showing several doorways
along one side.

She was about to retrace her steps, to find the door
through which she had entered the tavern, and from there
explore other paths which might lead her back to the
streets of town, and maybe to the curiosity shop standing at
the corner. It was then that one of the doors opened, and
the figure of a woman appeared. With the moonlight
behind her, her face was hidden; but Emma could see that
her shoulders were bent, and that she walked with the aid
of a stick that came tap-tapping along the corridor towards

her.

Hiding in the shadows against the wall, she watched the old woman pass by, and heard her muttering to herself. From the top of the stairs she called out to the scarred-faced man below; and the sound of her voice was like that of a crow calling from a tree-top. "Evan Du! . . . Evan Du! . . ." she croaked.

By and by he came to the foot of the stairs, and she beckoned him to come to her. After a murmured conversation, with much furtive pointing and chuckling one with the other, they parted company. Evan Du returned to his task of serving ale to thirsty visitors and subduing those the worse for drink, while the old woman made her way back along the corridor.

The moonlight now lit up her face, accentuating the lines drawn upon her cheeks and forehead. Her hair hung straight, streaked with grey, and her pursed lips turned down in an expression of surly displeasure. Emma shrank deeper into the shadows; but once more the woman passed her by as though she were part of them. At length she shuffled off into the room from which she had emerged, and shut the door behind her.

From the top of the stairs where the old woman had stood Emma could hear the swell of laughter and merry-making. It was there that another sound attracted her attention, a disquieting sound coming, not from the tavern below, but from somewhere overhead. Behind her, in a darkened recess at the end of the corridor, she noticed a narrow flight of steps leading up to the attic. It was from there that it came – the sobs and sighs of someone crying.

There was little purpose in her stealing up to the attic room, Emma remembered, for since she was an intruder in this scene of events long past, who could hear her footsteps?

She found the door open. There was no lamp burning inside. The window stood out against the sky, but the rest of the room was in darkness.

"You can't hear me, I know," Emma called out from the doorway. "It's sad to listen to your weeping. I wonder who you are, all alone in the dark. I wish there was something I could do to help you in your trouble. You see, I'm just a dreamer wandering past from a long time away."

It seemed only natural that no one should answer a ghost from some future time. However, just then the crying ceased, as though someone had sensed the presence of a stranger at the door. A moment later there was a glow inside the room as a match was struck and the candle lit. There, in the corner, a young boy was sitting up in bed. His eyes were opened wide, and tears still trickled down his cheeks as he stared towards the door. Emma turned with a start, thinking there was someone standing behind her of whom he was afraid. But it soon became clear that his eyes were fixed on her.

"Who's there?" he trembled.

Emma drew closer, tingling with excitement. "You can see me!" she cried.

The boy slid out of bed, retreating farther into the corner, his eyes following her every movement.

"You can!" she repeated. "You can hear my voice, and see me as clearly as I see you!"

He held the candle above his head and peered more closely. "Only faintly," he said. "Your voice seems far away. Who are you? Why have you come?"

Emma looked about the room. The ceiling was low, and the walls sloped away, following the angles of the roof. The floor was bare, with only the bed standing on the boards and a worn blanket draped upon it. There were no curtains hanging at the window. She looked out over the trees and the silver-bright pathway winding among them.

"Often and often I have watched the light burning in your window; and wondered who lived here in the attic room of Tŷ-yn-y-Cysgodion."

"Tŷ-yn-y-Cysgodion? . . . I don't understand." The boy had ventured from the corner, no longer afraid of the misty figure of a girl, little older than he. "There's nowhere for miles hereabouts – only the woods at Coed-y-Celyn, and farm-houses scattered around the hills."

"House in the Shadows . . ." Emma reflected. "That's how folk always remember this old house."

Standing there at the window, she looked along the moonlit path and beyond, where there were only woods and hills, clear to the horizon. Where were the streets of town, with her grandfather's curiosity shop standing at the corner, she wondered.

"Do you come from far away?" the boy asked, as though he were reading her thoughts.

"Not a long distance," Emma said absently, "but many, many years away."

For a while the boy pondered on her reply. He was beside her now, looking out over the distant hills. "I wish I were miles and miles from this place," he sighed wistfully. "Some day I will run and hide where they would never find me."

In the candle-light he noticed that the girl's translucent form was not reflected in the window pane, nor did it cast a shadow on the floor. "I wish I were a ghost, and could wander wherever I pleased. You are a ghost, aren't you?" he said to her in a half-frightened whisper.

"I'm really not sure," Emma answered, for all the while

she had wondered whether the house and all those within it
had come from the past to haunt her, or whether she had
journeyed backward in time to call upon them. But then,
she asked herself, weren't ghosts always dead and gone:
spirits who come to revisit places they once knew in their
erstwhile existence? "I don't think so," she added with
some conviction. "Perhaps this old house and all its people:
Evan Du, the old woman with the crooked back, even this
room where a young boy sleeps – perhaps none of you is
truly here at all!"

To see if he were real, Emma stretched out her hand to
touch the boy's hair, which tumbled over his forehead in
heavy locks, then his pallid cheeks. "You look so sad.
What were you crying for?"

He did not answer her for a while, and Emma could see
fresh tears glistening in his long, dark lashes. He looked
into her eyes, as though he were begging her to
understand.

"Some day I will run away," he said again, "when I find
somewhere they'll never discover me. You wouldn't believe
how cruel they can be – and how wicked too!"

He turned suddenly to look towards the door, listening
for footsteps on the stairs, afraid that he should see
someone standing there. But there was only the sound of
distant voices drifting up from downstairs.

For a long time Emma stayed to keep him company in
the attic room, until many drinkers began to leave the
tavern and make their way home; and others, who had
broken their journey to seek a night's rest, retired to their
beds. She stayed until the house was quiet and the candle
burned low, listening to the tale of a poor waif with no folk
of his own who had been given shelter by two old women –
distant relatives, the boy believed – who showed neither

love nor kindness. The story came tumbling from his lips.

"They gave me a bed . . . far away from the others . . . where I'm not seen or heard. And they give me food . . . only when they remember. From first light till long after dark I must work hard in the stables behind the tavern . . . tending the travellers' horses . . . and cleaning the stalls . . ."

He went on to describe how he was sent to gather fuel for the fire from the woods at Coed-y-Celyn, and made to do all the drudgery about the house, with surly commands and beatings when he was too tired to work harder; how once, when he ran away, he was pursued and captured by Evan Du, and locked in the cellar in the cold and dark. He lived in fear of this villain with a heart of stone, and the two old women who never seemed to sleep, but roamed the corridors long after nightfall. "I wish I could be far, far away from this horrid place," he ended with a sigh.

When at last he lay on the bed, his eyes were red with dark shadows beneath them, from crying and weariness.

"Don't go," he said pitifully. "Don't leave me."

Soon afterwards he fell asleep. And Emma sat on the floor beside his bed, resting her head on the blanket and laying her arm upon his. He seemed so lonely lying there.

CHAPTER 5

". . . I was really there! . . ."

Perhaps Emma, too, had fallen asleep, for she could remember no more of her conversation with the boy in the attic room. How long she had stayed there with him she could not tell. Maybe she had sat beside his bed with her head upon the blanket for hours and hours. Yet now, when she opened her eyes, the boy, the bed where he had lain – even the room itself – had vanished. She found herself back in the curiosity shop, with the lamp-light shining on the picture of the old tavern; and the clocks ticking away on the shelves and in the window had, only moments ago, spelled out the hour of eight. However long her journey had taken, not a minute of the time had been measured by them.

Emma looked around, bewildered. "It couldn't all have been a dream!" she whispered, staring into the shadows under the porch where she had sheltered from the thunder-storm. "I was really there!" How else could she remember so vividly each moment of that strange adventure: a sky ablaze with streaks of light, the piercing eyes of Evan Du, an old woman who shuffled along the corridor and beckoned him from above the stairs, and the boy, alone in the attic room, who had told of his fears and sadness. She could still hear his voice begging her to stay.

"I was there – I truly was!" she determined; for she knew that neither dreams nor imagination could conjure up such visions. From her reflection in the darkened window she saw that her hair and clothing were in no way bedraggled by the rain. And most mysterious of all was how those stolen hours had passed unnoticed by her grandfather's clocks.

During supper Emma was quiet. She was longing to tell of her odd experience, but was sure no one would believe her; for whenever she began to disclose her dreams, or ramble on with stories of make-believe, her grandmother always shook her head or closed her eyes and breathed a long sigh.

Tucked up in her bed that night, Emma's thoughts wandered back to the boy, frightened and miserable and alone. But when she fell asleep she did not dream of him. Her dreams were of fleeing through the woods at Coed-y-Celyn: running on and on to escape the clutches of a scarred-faced man who was close at her heels. And whichever way she turned, an old woman with a crooked back stood in her path, screeching with laughter. Many times she woke with a start.

The following afternoon her grandfather was busy at his work-bench when Emma came home from school. All day long her thoughts had been far away, and there was no one with whom she could share them. Friends would think her demented if she were to describe an adventure in a house now fallen to ruin, and an encounter with sinister folk who lived there in the past.

She looked over his shoulder at the assortment of wheels and springs gathered around him. "Grandad . . ." she began, with some hestitation, "a long time ago, when the shadowy house near the woods at Coed-y-Celyn . . . when it was a tavern, sheltering travellers on their journey to Ireland . . . why were folk afraid to stay there through the night?"

For a while the old man was engrossed in his work, and made no reply. Then, at length, he raised his head and said to her: "That was all so long ago, and best forgotten now."

"But you must remember the stories that you were told."

He fell silent, reminiscing it seemed: once again remembering tales he would never tell.

"Was it the old woman who lived there they were afraid of?" She lowered her voice to a whisper. "Was she a witch?"

Emma waited eagerly for her grandfather to unfold further mysteries of the shadowy house. Instead, he returned to his tinkering with the springs and shiny wheels, and seemed little inclined to recall the tales of days gone by.

Emma was watching him from the corner of her eye, wondering how best to relate the story of her enchanted journey backwards through the years. That it was too incredible for him to believe, she could well understand. But she wondered also if it were truly Tŷ-yn-y-Cysgodion that had come to haunt her, or had she found herself in some eerie place which crept from the depths of her imagination?

"Sometimes – in my dreams, I mean –" she ventured, "sometimes I go back to that old house, and wander around inside, as though I were a traveller of long ago, looking for a place to shelter. In my dreams I steal up to the doorway under the porch and peep inside, and I see it all just as it used to be . . . ."

"My Beautiful Dreamer," the old man smiled, without raising his eyes from his delicate task.

"Men and women are gathered there in the lamp-light, laughing and singing and drinking ale from large mugs," Emma went on. "One night I dreamed I passed by a cruel-looking man with a scar across his cheek. He was standing so close that I could gaze into his eyes; just as close as I am standing to you!"

She held out her hand to touch her grandfather's shoulder, and noticed that he was not smiling any longer.

"Evan Du he was called," she said.

Emma could feel her heart beating faster. She knew now that it was not an imaginary place where she had chanced to wander. It was truly the tavern at Coed-y-Celyn that she had come upon. Why else would her grandfather look so startled at the mention of Evan Du?

"A strange name. It's likely you have told me of the scarred-faced man before," she hastened to explain. "That was why I remembered him in my dreams.

"Then I climbed stairs which led to a long corridor, where I saw an old woman shuffling towards me. And when she drew close I hid myself in the shadows against the wall. I don't know why I should have been afraid of her. She could never see me, for I was only there in my dreams."

"If dreams of that bleak old house still keep you from your sleep," her grandfather said, "I'm sorry the picture was ever returned."

As the evening wore on, Emma thought more and more about the boy in the attic room, wondering if she would ever see him again. She recalled how forlorn he was: how tears welled up in his eyes as he begged her not to leave him. But she remembered, too, the furtiveness of Evan Du and the old woman as they muttered together above the stairs, and wondered what mischief they had contrived.

Later that evening, before the lamps of the curiosity shop were put out, Emma looked into her picture. For a while she could not quite understand how the scene had changed. Through the trees the silver-bright pathway wound its way to the porch; swathes of ivy clung to the walls; the moon was still shining in the sky. Yet somehow the house was different. There was something about it which was strangely unfamiliar. The doorway was hidden in the shadows as it had always been; and the windows . . . "The windows – yes, that's it!" Emma breathed. "There is no light burning in the attic window!"

Was it some ill-omen? she wondered. Had something happened to the boy? If only she could have stayed with him a little while longer. Perhaps she might have helped him escape from the two women and a scarred-faced man who kept him prisoner there.

When the last lamp was turned out, she groped her way through the darkness to the foot of the stairs. Her grandfather was ahead of her, and had almost reached the landing.

"Sometimes dreams are so vivid that they don't seem like dreams at all," she called after him.

Her voice resounded – louder somehow, and prolonged with echoes – as though she were calling to him through a bare room with a high ceiling. She became aware of the bannister rail, unfamiliar to her touch, and the sound of the old man's footsteps ahead of her on the stairs – heavier and quicker than they usually were.

At the top of the stairs Emma found a corridor stretching before her, with the window at the far end through which the moonlight came slanting in. She stifled a cry of alarm when she noticed that it was not her grandfather whom she followed. If he were to turn around, and if his face were not hidden from the moonlight, she knew she would see the scarred cheek and piercing eyes of Evan Du!

Along the corridor he went, treading more stealthily now. Then he stopped at the door from which the old woman had emerged, and knocked upon it softly.

"Agatha," he called in a subdued voice, as though he wished to disturb no one else. And then again, more urgently: "Agatha! Open the door!"

A glow of lamp-light spilled out as the door was opened. There was a muttering in the doorway, and Evan Du went in.

Emma did not stop to listen. Instead, she made her way back along the corridor and up the flight of steps which led to the attic room. There was no chink of light showing beneath the door.

"Who's there?" the boy called when he heard someone knocking.

"It's Emma. I've come back again," she whispered, fearing that someone else might hear her.

After a while the door opened, and Emma heard a sleepy voice coming from inside the room.

"Emma? . . . I didn't know your name – only that you come from a long time away. I must have fallen asleep. Remember? You were sitting on the floor beside my bed . . ." He lit the candle, looking at her with his eyes half closed. "You promised you would stay."

Emma could only stare and wonder – wonder at the capricious rhythm of time. For here in this Otherworld twenty-four hours had rushed by in almost as many moments, while on her grandfather's clocks not a second of it was recorded. In her confusion, she imagined that past time was pursuing the present, and that some day they would merge as one.

"That was last night – hours and hours ago!" she told him, but with little conviction, because even now his eyes were misty with tears, and the candle still burned low.

With the candle-stick held high, the boy edged his way full circle around her, searching for a shadow, whispering her name over and over, wondering perhaps if she had come to him in a dream. "Emma . . . Emma . . ." he breathed. "The light is passing clear through you, and shining on the wall. I thought ghosts were always withered and frightful – not young and pretty with golden hair."

"What's your name?" Emma asked, feeling uneasy.

"John – as far as I remember," he answered. "But usually they call me 'Foundling' or 'Little Devil'!" He grinned mischievously. "I call him 'Black Heart' and them 'The Two Witches' – under my breath, that is. You would never believe how wicked they can be! I dare not tell, or I should be buried in the cellar where no one would ever find me!"

Emma shuddered. "I found Evan Du stealing along the corridor – only a little while ago. He knocked on a door and called to someone named Agatha. Before he went in they were whispering together. Is she the old woman with a crooked back?"

"Agatha and Jessie," the boy muttered. "They're as black-hearted as Evan Du! It is likely they are plotting some devilry. You would never believe how cunning they are! You shall see for yourself."

He blew out the candle, and led the way down over the steps from the attic to the corridor below. "We must be quiet, and keep out of sight," he warned. "Jessie and Agatha have sharp eyes, and ears that never miss a sound!"

"They can never see me, nor hear my footsteps," Emma said, remembering how closely they had passed her by without so much as glancing in her direction.

The corridor was still lit by shafts of moonlight, with no one now in sight. There was no sound from downstairs, for the local farmers who frequented the tavern had returned to their homes; and travellers resting overnight had retired to their beds.

Together they roamed the shadowy stairs and passages, peeping around corners, listening at doorways, startled at every creak of the boards.

"All through the night they prowl about," John whispered, "like foxes searching for prey. Sometimes I hear voices crying out . . ."

He stopped abruptly, and tip-toed away to hide in the darkest corner when they heard footsteps approaching. Then a glimmer appeared to light the way of someone coming down the stairs. Emma recognised the tall figure of Evan Du, carrying on his shoulder some very heavy burden. Behind him came the tap-tapping of Agatha's walking stick; and beside her, holding a lamp, was a gaunt woman whom Emma had never seen before.

A voice kept whispering in Emma's thoughts: "Don't be afraid. They can never see you, for you're not really here at all. It's only a dream, only an echo of long ago."

Yet she began to tremble as they came close.

CHAPTER 6

. . . "Witches!" he cried
. . .

Down the stairs they came, and past the counter upon which the casks of ale lay, moving along the tavern floor, silent and solemn as bearers at a funeral. The women looked quite unlike sisters, for while Agatha bent low, leaning on her stick, Jessie was lean and stood erect. The only similarities were their tight lips and eyes deep-set in hollows shaded from the lamplight.

They passed close by, and Emma let out a cry of fright when she saw, hanging limp at the back of Evan Du, the head and arms of a body slung over his shoulder. So shrill was her cry that Jessie looked back, as though it had startled her. She stopped for a moment, and the light shone on Emma's face.

"What was that?" Emma heard her say. They listened for a moment longer, the gaunt woman moving the lamp from side to side, groping in the darkness. Emma backed away, fearful that Jessie, too, might be aware of her presence.

"There's no one," croaked the sister with the crooked back. "Everybody's fast asleep."

They moved on across the room; but after every few steps Jessie glanced over her shoulder, muttering about a cry she fancied she had heard. Then they turned into a passage-way leading towards the back of the house, and went out of sight.

Emma searched about, calling softly: "John! . . . John, where are you?"

Presently, he came from his hiding place and stood at her side. His voice trembled. "They're taking him down to the cellar," he said. "No one will find him there! He'll be just another traveller, lost on his journey."

Emma stared after them, at the glow of the lamp growing faint along the passage.

"Is he . . . dead?"

"Murdered in his bed, I shouldn't wonder!" the boy whispered, "and all his money and belongings stolen!"

Emma felt faint with horror. "No – they couldn't have!" she cried incredulously. Then she closed her eyes, longing to awaken from this nightmare.

"It's happened before," the boy went on. "When the house is quiet I've heard their footsteps going down the stairs – sometimes a voice crying out! I was too frightened to follow." He moved closer to Emma. "I'm not so afraid while you are with me," he added bravely.

"No one could be so evil!" Emma was saying over and over again.

There was no light to guide them as they followed in the footsteps of Evan Du and the old women; but the boy knew his way in the dark. "Don't go too near them," he continued. "They say Jessie and Agatha have the second sight, and can hear every sound!"

They came to an open door at the end of the passage, and from there a flight of steps led down to the cellar. That was where the gruesome task was performed. Jessie still held the lamp, while Evan Du dug into the cellar floor until a shallow grave was fashioned there. The body lay sprawled on the ground beside it, and as Emma and John peered from the top of the steps they noticed its deathly grimace and eyes that stared up, never seeing the lamplight.

"They're going to bury him there!" the boy whispered.

Emma could only watch, and tremble at the horror of it all.

At length, they made their way back to the room in the attic, where the boy bolted the door behind them. "We shall be safe here," he said. "Don't be afraid."

He need have no fear for her safety, Emma reflected with growing courage. After all, wasn't she just someone from a long time away, and this summer night just a grisly chapter from some story of the past?

"If I were here with you always," she told him, "then perhaps we could run away together – somewhere they would never find us."

John looked at her wistfully. "Oh, Emma . . . if only we could!" Then, after a moment's reflection, his troubled expression was back again. "Wherever I hide, they will seek me out. However far I go, he will come to fetch me."

"You can't stay in this awful place!" Emma said earnestly. "Tŷ-yn-y-Cysgodion – House in the Shadows – that's how everyone remembers it. They will never forget the two old women and their wickedness. My grandfather says that long ago . . ."

Her voice trailed away, and she looked at him in bewilderment, for she realised that there was nothing she could do to alter the path of destiny. And although time seemed to leap backwards and forwards mysteriously, past events could never be changed. The house was now really gone. Evan Du and the old women – they all lay mouldering in their graves. Even the boy must now have grown old: so old that likely he had died as well.

But as he looked at her with his sad eyes – as he stood there so helpless – then all reflections of the past melted away. Instead, she began to wonder how she was going to find her way back to her grandparents and the curiosity shop: to the time where she belonged. And maybe, she thought – although the notion seemed too absurd even to dwell on – maybe, if they searched for a way, the boy could make the journey with her.

"We will wait until the daylight comes," she told him.

The night wore on as they talked together in the candle-light. Emma listened to tales of Evan Du, of lone travellers, occasionally packmen who bought and sold their merchandise and transported it by mule to the market places of the north. Weary and thirsty after their journey, they drank heartily at the tavern and fell into sound sleep from which some poor souls were never to awaken. "You know now why they will never be seen again," the boy explained grimly.

His eyes opened wide with wonder when Emma told of the cobbled streets of town, where throngs of people wandered about among the shops and tall buildings, all standing close together. She drew for him an image of her grandfather's curiosity shop, arrayed with a variety of clocks that ticked and chimed and measured all the hours of the day and night, of its walls and shelves aglitter with a thousand adornments. All this she described, and many novelties besides – the world of a later century which he could never have dreamed of.

The boy tingled with excitement as he pictured the scenes she portrayed. "If only I were a ghost," he sighed. "Then we could go there together."

"There must be a way," said Emma. "When daylight comes we will go far and farther still, until we find a place where this old house is just a memory."

Early in the morning, when the grey light of dawn first showed in the sky, Emma looked from the window of the attic room at the woodland wrapped in mist, and the hill-tops on the horizon edged with gold. When their talking was over, the boy had lain on his bed and slept fitfully while she kept watch for daybreak. Now he was sitting up, rubbing his eyes sleepily. He seemed glad that she should still be there to keep him company.

"Is it time? Has the daylight come?" he asked. Then he went to the door, quietly unfastened the bolt and listened for any sign of movement downstairs. The house was still.

"We shall have to steal away. Agatha and Jessie . . . they hear every sound!"

So, with furtive glances all about, they made their way down over the stairs and along silent passages, making their escape through a back door which led to a cobbled yard. In the middle of the yard was a carriage, with its shafts resting on the ground; and beyond were the woodshed and stables. Horses whinnied and scuffed their hooves restively as they passed by.

The path curled around the house to the front porch, and then wound its way through the trees in the direction from which Emma had first approached. Her heart leapt when, in the distance, she fancied she saw rows of houses with smoke drifting from the chimneys.

"Come along – this way!" she urged, running ahead, for soon they would come to the streets of town and find the curiosity shop standing at the corner.

But as they drew nearer, the roof-tops changed to foliage tumbling against the sky, with the morning mist swirling among the highest branches. The trees closed in around them, and they found themselves in a wood where the grey of the sky turned to shadowy green. Here the dawn chorus was in full song and woodpeckers were tapping in the boughs. Once in a while the boy looked back, fearing that he should hear heavy footfalls and see a figure dressed all in black close at his heels.

"When they find I'm gone, they'll send Evan Du to search about and drag me back again!" the boy said when they stopped to catch their breath. "Wherever I hide they will find me!"

On and on they went, farther and farther from Tŷ-yn-y-Cysgodion, until the sun had risen higher in the sky and its rays filtered down through the trees. With no paths to follow, there was only the sunlight to guide them on their way.

"He could never follow our footprints, weaving among the twigs and fallen leaves," Emma assured him. But in her heart she was afraid that although they wandered long and far, through the woods and over the hills beyond, they would never come upon some enchanted bridge or rainbow that would lead to a place which might be a hundred years away.

When they were tired they rested in a clearing where a mossy bank made a soft pillow for their heads. The boy sat up and looked at his companion lying beside him.

"Emma . . ." he began, peering closer, "when the sun shines upon you, you become so faint that I could believe that you're not really there at all!"

"I wonder . . ." said Emma absently, gazing up into a patch of blue sky which seemed to go on forever, "I wonder if tomorrow is to the east or west or somewhere far away out there."

John seemed more anxious about the direction from which his pursuer might approach, for he was watching every shady nook in the woods around him; but nothing was stirring there.

"If it were in my dreams I travelled here," Emma mused, "then only while I am asleep can I find my way back to the time where I belong."

Often she closed her eyes, and kept them shut tightly for a minute or more, only to find that when she opened them again she still lay in a clearing in the woods with the boy beside her.

"Maybe this time I have run so fast and so far that he has given up the chase," John supposed. "He cannot search for me forever."

While they rested there, absorbed in their own thoughts, they hadn't noticed how quiet the woods had become. The birds had stopped singing, and there was no rustle of leaves or flutter of wings.

It was when they rose from the bank to continue their journey that they saw, among the trees behind them, the figure of a woman with bent shoulders, leaning on her stick. She waited there, not moving, but holding them in her stare.

"Agatha!" they cried out together.

And as they watched, another figure appeared from behind the trees nearby. It was Jessie, the gaunt sister, and she beckoned the boy to come to them.

Frightened, they ran on as fast as their legs would carry them. And as they ran they wondered by what sorcery two old women had been able to overtake them.

It was a long while before they dared look around to see if they were being pursued; and now there was no sign of Agatha and Jessie behind them. Instead, they saw two crows flying low beneath the trees, and then perching on a bough, so close that they could see the shine of the birds' feathers and hear their raucous crying.

"You see . . ." said John, fighting for his breath, "there's nowhere . . . nowhere we can hide from them!"

Then, to Emma's astonishment, he flung a broken branch up into the tree, and shouted as the birds fluttered and squawked.

"Witches!" he cried, half in fear and half in rage. "Go away, and leave me alone!"

They struggled on, almost too exhausted to run any farther. Looking back, they saw the crows at once take flight, swooping down from their perch and circling about them, wings entangled in their hair. The birds dived and soared, tormenting them, until at length Emma and John came to a brook stretching across their path.

They stumbled through the water and climbed the bank on the other side. There, for some unaccountable reason, the crows were loath to follow. For a while they circled overhead. The next moment they were gone.

Their eyes searched the sky and the shade under the trees.

"We're safe from them here," John sighed. "They say that witches can follow God-fearing folk no farther than the middle of the next running stream."

Emma did not share his relief, for looking back across the brook, among the trees where they had passed, she saw Jessie and Agatha staring at them – wondering perhaps how they could cross the water.

CHAPTER 7

. . . Never would she part with it . . .

Agatha and Jessie came from among the trees, but dared not venture across the running brook. They stood on the bank, with their arms stretched forward, as though they were reaching out to clutch at them.

John and Emma seized their chance to escape, and as they ran off they heard their pursuers calling after them: "Come back! There's nowhere you can hide. Little Devil – come back!"

And then a deeper fear crept into Emma's heart, for now a voice was calling to her. "Emma . . . Emma . . ." it called, with an urgency she could not understand. "Emma, where are you? I know you're there."

In all her wanderings among the haunts and the folk of long ago, it was only the boy who ever sensed her presence: only he to whom she was visible. Now, by their witchcraft, had the old women found her, too? "Emma . . ." the voice kept echoing. "Where are you?"

Then, with a cry of fright, she found that the wood around her had been plunged into darkness.

"Come along Emma," she heard again. It was some time before she realised that it was her grandfather calling to her from the top of the stairs. "I couldn't see you down there in the dark," he said as she climbed up towards him.

In the living room above the curiosity shop, Emma stood in the hearth, pale and trembling. She took her grandfather's arm and buried her head in his chest to hide her tears. It was as though she had been on a long journey and was thankful to be home again. Who would believe she had travelled a hundred years, and wandered for a night and a day in her Otherworld, in as many moments as it takes for the clocks to chime the hour. It was almost too fantastic an adventure for her to believe herself.

"Why, you're cold and trembling, my love!" the old man said, drawing a chair close to the fire. "Sit here and warm yourself a while."

Mrs Dalamore placed her hand on Emma's brow and breathed out a long sigh. "You've caught a chill, I shouldn't wonder. With this bitter east wind it's as cold as a tomb downstairs!"

After supper she was put straight to bed, with a draught of medicine to cool her fever, and an extra blanket laid over her. For a long time she lay awake, recalling each memory of Tŷ-yn-y-Cysgodion. She was glad to have escaped from that fearful house: from the clutches of Evan Du and the old sisters from whom it seemed no secrets could be hidden. But she was sorry to have left the boy, frightened and alone: to have deserted him when he so wanted a friend to give him courage. Now it would be growing dark, she imagined; and he would be wandering through the woods, watching, listening – startled at every sound, and not knowing which path to take.

"If only I could have stayed a while longer," she whispered under her breath; "until the daylight had gone, and Jessie and Agatha were left far behind . . ."

It was clear to her now that longing or dreaming would not make it so. She was more and more inclined to believe that the house had a will and a heart of its own, and called whenever it wished her there. Perhaps it emerged from the past the moment it beckoned, lingered a spell, and then crumbled to dust when she went away. It was never she who chose the time to come and go.

When Emma fell asleep, the shadowy house and those who once lived there were still in her thoughts; and they returned when she woke up the following morning.

Later that day there came about a turn of events which, had they run their course, might have ended forever Emma's journeys to the house near the woods at Coed-y-Celyn. Evan Du and the forbidding sisters would, in time, have become just a memory; and gone, too, would be Emma's friend – the boy with sad eyes and heavy locks tumbling over his forehead.

Her grandmother had decided that she was not well enough to attend school. So, having lain in bed during the morning, she was now allowed to wrap up warmly and keep her grandfather company downstairs. As usual, he was tinkering with his clocks, while Emma was left to welcome anyone who came to browse around the curiosity shop.

The light was fading, and Emma was lighting the lamps, when the bell above the door tinkled. A woman stood in the doorway, accompanied by a boy who stared about him at the glittering array of curios. He passed from one to another, his eyes wide with interest: at the music boxes which Emma rewound, at clocks with cuckoo calls and pendulums that wagged against the wall, at quaint ornaments, and collections of lead soldiers parading in scarlet and gold. Each object that caught his attention was examined with enthusiasm.

The woman smiled patiently as she followed the boy around. "Perhaps you could suggest a gift for my son's birthday," she said. "He is fond of things which are old and curious. Whenever we are passing by he stops to gaze into the window."

With a gesture, Emma invited them to search among the shelves until they found something which pleased him.

Presently, the boy's attention was drawn to the pictures on the wall, and when his eyes fell upon the the shadowy house standing in the moonlight, it seemed that for a moment he was held spellbound, just as Emma had been when first she had wiped away the dust and brought the picture into the lamplight.

The boy moved closer, staring up at it.

"It looks like a haunted house from a story book!" he murmured. "See how the light shines in the window as a ghost roams the empty rooms! And there's a full moon," he went on, pointing to the sky. "Ghosts are always about when the moon is bright! If you stare hard and long at the window, you can see the light flickering . . ."

"It's just an old house," Emma interrupted, for she was anxious to distract the boy's attention from what was now her most treasured possession. "You can never believe all the stories people tell. Besides, you would soon get tired of looking at a lonely house in the moonlight."

"Perhaps it's the ghost of someone who lived there long ago," the boy surmised, still wondering and staring at the light in the attic window. "Look, Mother. Look how eerie it is, hidden away in the shadows!"

"Whatever gift you choose, you shall have," the woman smiled indulgently. "But isn't it rather dark and gloomy?"

"It would give you nightmares, I shouldn't wonder," Emma reflected. But the mystery of clouds sweeping across the sky; of a wind that stirred the trees and sighed mournfully – all these memories she kept secret.

The boy's eyes were bright with excitement. "I could hang it in my room," he said; "and watch all day long until the light flickers again. Then maybe I shall see the ghost passing by the window!"

"No! I must never part with it!" a despairing voice cried out in Emma's thoughts; for she knew that if the boy should take the picture away, the spell would be broken. John would be left alone, with no one to help or give him courage. She might never see him again.

"It's just a painting of an old house," she told them once more. "It lay in the cellar for a long time, and the colours are fading. If you were to touch it, the canvas would crumble, I shouldn't wonder."

Tinkering with his clocks not far away, old Mr Dalamore chuckled to himself as he listened to his granddaughter's wiles. He knew full well that with her beguiling talk and frank, blue eyes, there were few who could resist her persuasion.

"There are so many things to choose from," Emma explained. "They are all more exciting than the picture of a dreary house that never moves nor makes a sound."

She showed them a variety of pocket watches and clockwork toys and knives in leather sheaths. But the boy gave them only a cursory glance, time and again being drawn to the picture of the shadowy house.

"It's faded and dreary, I know; but he has his heart set on it," the woman sighed, surprised at the fascination it seemed to hold for the boy. "I promised he should choose something for himself."

Emma wore her most sombre expression as she stood beside them, looking up into the picture of Tŷ-yn-y-Cysgodion.

"As far as I know, it lay for a long time forgotten in the

darkness of the cellar," she repeated; "ever since my grandfather was a young man, I'm told. Once upon a time folk believed that the house was haunted; but that was long ago, and it's likely the tales were never true. The picture has a curse upon it, I've heard."

Emma laughed with derision; yet the woman and her son listened intently.

"Since the dust and cobwebs were wiped away and it has hung here in the lamplight," Emma went on, "I found nothing strange about it – until one night when I was alone . . ."

"You noticed the light in the window flickering!" the boy interrupted, pointing to the attic room.

"It's more mysterious than that," Emma replied.

And not far away, old Mr Dalamore, tinkering with his cogs and wheels, was smiling to himself, for he knew well that once his granddaughter's imagination was set alight it could burn more fiercely than a forest fire.

Emma's eyes were twinkling in the lamplight. "Perhaps I should tell you the story from the beginning – just as it was told long ago . . ." She began to recall an old Welsh legend her grandfather had heard when he was a boy.

"This old manor house was once the home of a man of the church – a rector I believe he was – who lived there alone, for he had no children and his wife had been dead many a year.

"It all began one night when he was walking along the corridor on his way to bed. He could hardly believe his eyes when there appeared before him the figure of a lady dressed in white. She was drifting silently along, and then, just as suddenly as she came, she vanished in the shadows!"

The boy's eyes moved from Emma to the picture and back again. His face was pale as ivory.

Emma lowered her voice. "At first he thought a shaft of moonlight had come slanting through the window and played tricks with his imagination. But the next night and many more times that summer, the figure of the White Lady came from nowhere to haunt the rooms of the manor. Each time he saw her she became more real and more frightful. Not now a misty shape, but a woman with hollow cheeks and burning eyes. And whenever she appeared he heard a sound like the murmur of a heart-beat which grew loud and louder still, until it echoed through the house. They say that the furniture trembled and the curtains swayed from side to side.

"Always after nightfall she came; and never in the same place. Sometimes he saw her moving along the corridor, sometimes on the stairs. Once he woke to find her standing at the foot of his bed!

"At last he could stand it no longer. So at the first sound of the ghost approaching – the first murmur of a heart-beat – he would flee from the house and hide in the woods. And there he would stay until the ghost had gone. Even then he could hardly find enough courage to venture back indoors, for there were no neighbours to keep him company."

"Does the White Lady go there still?" the boy asked in a half-frightened whisper.

"The house has fallen to ruin, long before we were born. It's only a tale the old people tell."

The boy fell silent, and his mother glanced at him nervously.

"The old rector lived in fear of nightfall," Emma continued. "Then, one evening, a gipsy woman called at the house, selling her rush mats and coloured ribbons. When the door opened she looked at the rector standing there, and her eyes wandered past him into the dusky hall.

At once she was frightened, and clutched her basket in her arms, and stepped back from the threshold.

"'Ysbrydion . . . Ysbrydion!' she muttered, for she could sense an evil presence in the house."

"Ghosts!" the boy whispered.

It was then that Emma began to wonder whether her capricious story was making him more enchanted with the shadowy house or filling his thoughts with apprehension. Perhaps she should simply explain that the picture had been given to her, and that never, never would she part with it. But she had promised always to be helpful and courteous to customers who came to look around the curiosity shop. She continued her story in as mysterious a tone as she could effect.

"The rector followed her out under the porch, because he knew that gipsies had a strange understanding of ghosts and their haunting ways. There he learned of an old gipsy remedy with which he might rid the house of the spirit. The White Lady, she told him, would have to be put to the test of the bell and candle."

The boy looked puzzled. "The bell and candle?" he frowned.

"Around the parishes in the county the rector searched until he found twelve men of the church," Emma explained. "Then, on a certain night, they gathered together around a table in the attic room of the manor house. And upon the table twelve handbells and twelve candles were placed.

"According to the gipsy's story, ghosts always seek the darkness and are angered by the pealing of bells. So when the hour of midnight approached, the candles were to be lit and the handbells rung. The ghost, she told him, would brave the noise of the bells and try with all her might to blow out the candles which broke the darkness. If every flame was blown out before the twelfth stroke of the clock, then the ghost could never be driven away, and the house would remain haunted forever. But if just one flame still burned, then the ghost would be banished from the house, never to return.

"Midnight came. Then they heard the sound of heart-beats growing as loud as thunder. A wind howled in the corridors, and the whole house seemed to tremble as the White Lady approached.

"The clock began to strike . . ."

Just then the clocks in the curiosity shop struck the passing of the hour. The boy jumped with fright, and his mother held him close.

"A flowing white gown and the fiery eyes of the ghost appeared! In a rage she rushed among them blowing out the candles while the men of the church rang the handbells and chanted prayers. The louder they rang the bells and raised their voices, the more furious she became, until her breath was as fierce as the wind in the corridors.

"At the last stroke of midnight, every flame had been extinguished, and the attic room was in darkness."

Emma watched the boy closely.

"So the ghost would stay there forever!" he declared.

"The night you were alone," the woman remembered, "when something mysterious happened?"

"Oh, yes," Emma recalled. "That night, while I was turning out the lamps, I heard my heart beating. Then it grew louder and louder still, above the ticking of the clocks, until all the ornaments on the shelves and the pictures on the walls began to tremble at the sound of it. And when I looked up at the painting of the old manor house . . ." She lowered her voice to a whisper. "For a little while, strange to say, the light in the attic window went out!"

CHAPTER 8

". . . I won't leave you . . ."

When Emma's story was over, the woman and her son remained silent for a while, looking first at each other and then at the picture of Tŷ-yn-y-Cysgodion above them in the lamplight.

"It's just as though the ghost of the lady dressed all in white was here in the room!" the boy said incredulously.

"Sometimes," Emma answered, confident now that he would never dare hang the picture in his room. "Perhaps only when the moon is bright."

"You would be tormented by horrid dreams all through the night," his mother decided, her tone no longer indulgent.

She looked around at the other pictures hanging there; and the boy looked with her, once in a while allowing his eyes to wander back to the shadowy house bathed in moonlight, perhaps listening for the murmur of a heart-beat growing louder.

After much searching, the boy chose a painting of an autumn scene, where hounds and horses and huntsmen in their scarlet coats gathered under the morning sun.

"It's more colourful than a dreary old house," Emma told him, pointing out the golden foliage of the trees and the delicate blue of the sky. And with a smile she added:

"It's likely the White Lady would be furious if we were to disturb her! There are so many old paintings that have stories told about them."

They promised to call again one day, and before they left the curiosity shop the boy stole a lingering glance at the haunted manor house.

When they had gone, the old man shook his head in mild reproach. "My Beautiful Dreamer," he said. "One of these dark nights the door of Tŷ-yn-y-Cysgodion will open wide and we shall lose you forever!"

Emma smiled. Little did her grandfather suspect that his foretelling might well come to pass, she thought: that one day she would wander off into the Otherworld and never find her way back.

"The stories come to me while I lie in bed, before I go to sleep," she told him, "and sometimes they linger on in my dreams. Last night . . ."

She went on to tell him how – in her dreams, she was careful to say – she had found herself once more in the House of Shadows; how she had come upon a wretched boy, alone in an attic room. "Sometimes he runs away," she said; "but always the old women – the Devil Sisters I call them – always they find his hiding place by their witchery and send the black-hearted man with a scarred face to drag him back again!"

She described how she had seen them moving along the corridor and down over the stairs; told of their gruesome mission in the cellar. "The body was laid in the grave and buried under the ground!" she recalled.

The old man fell silent. Already he was startled at Emma's recollections, echoing so vividly events of the past which he had never dared speak of.

"Then, when daylight came, and we stole away into the

woods . . ." she was saying. But he was not listening any longer. He was remembering the tales of devilry which had spread throughout the county before the tavern had mouldered away: when the names of Tŷ-yn-y-Cysgodion and Evan Du and the Devil Sisters were whispered abroad. Perhaps the old man was afraid that somehow their ghosts had come back from the grave to haunt Emma's dreams.

Later that night, while Emma was asleep, he took the picture from the wall of the curiosity shop and put it back in the cellar where it had lain in years gone by.

"In time she will forget all about it," Mrs Dalamore assured him. "It's not natural for a girl's thoughts to dwell so much on fearful stories of long ago."

However, as the weeks passed by, there was scarcely a day when Emma did not remember the shadowy house and the folk she had met there. Memories of Evan Du and the Devil Sisters were engraved on her mind. And the boy secluded in the attic room, who feared them more than she – how could she ever forget him!

Often, while her grandfather was busy mending his clocks, she would steal down to the cellar and look into the picture, wondering and wondering. Always the trees and sky were still, with never a soul emerging from under the porch. But then, she remembered, hadn't the house a magic of its own, beckoning her at its will? However she longed to return to her friend in that Othertime, it was never she who determined when to come and go.

Alone in the darkness below the cellar stairs, she would sometimes hold the candle close, as though she could light up the shadows. "John . . . John . . ." she would call softly, so that no one upstairs should hear her voice and scorn her foolish day-dreams. But of course she never

71

heard the boy calling back to her, nor saw him appear in the attic window.

The spring wore on and the days grew longer. Emma's secret visits to the cellar became less frequent, until at length she hardly went there at all. That Otherworld of Evan Du and the Devil Sisters – even the boy who lived in fear of them – were all fading from her thoughts. And when the sun was shining brightly she was able to forget about them altogether, for always she associated Tŷ-yn-y-Cysgodion with moonlight and shadows and dark mystery, just as it was portrayed in the picture.

It was a fine morning, late on in spring. The sunlight came streaming through the windows of the curiosity shop and the ornaments were gleaming gold and silver. Emma was polishing and arranging the curios on the shelves when she had occasion to visit the cellar to store away some unwanted wares.

She approached the door which led down to the cellar; and with each step she took, the door seemed to draw farther away. Stranger still was the awning which appeared overhead, shutting out the sunlight in the room and throwing back echoes of her footsteps, as though she were moving along an underground passage, with an ever-receding door at the end of it. After a while it began to reverse the direction of its movement, and was now coming forward until it loomed large directly in front of her.

The door opened, and Emma let out a cry of fright when she saw at the threshold the figure of a woman with a crooked back, leaning on her stick. It was Agatha who stood there; and peering over her shoulder was the other sister – the gaunt, forbidding Jessie!

Every instinct urged Emma to run away; but she became

numbed with fear. Beyond the two old women she glimpsed the beams spanning the ceiling of the tavern, and the tables and chairs strewn around the walls. There was no sound of merriment and raised voices, for now the tavern was deserted, and the open shutters were letting in the daylight.

"Come inside," Agatha croaked, opening the door wider.

"It will soon be dusk," said Jessie. "Are you seeking food and rest for the night? Come, warm yourself beside the fire."

"We are so cold and hungry," came the reply from outside. Yet it was not Emma's voice that answered them: it was not she to whom the Devil Sisters beckoned. As far as they were aware, Emma was not there at all. Their eyes were looking right through her, at someone else who was standing beyond the threshold.

Astonished, Emma turned to see a young woman and a child waiting there, and behind them, instead of sunlight streaming through the windows of the curiosity shop, she saw a pathway lined with trees all muffled in snow. Some spell had summoned her back to the shadowy house, for it was there under the awning at its door that she found herself, on a cold afternoon in winter.

"You are very kind," the young woman was saying. "If only I can rest a while; and a bite to eat for the boy."

The sisters looked curiously at the mother and child, dressed in the clothes of gipsy folk, who had come knocking at their door. Many times afterwards Emma wondered why the old women had invited them in. It was clear they had neither money nor belongings to steal. Perhaps sometimes their cold hearts showed compassion, or else they were hatching some wicked plot.

"Come inside. Rest at the fire for a while," they said again.

So into the tavern they went – the visitors from the hills around who came begging for food and shelter, and with them a girl from some Othertime whom no one knew was there. Taking the child by the hand, the gipsy woman followed Jessie and Agatha to the *simne fawr,* the wide hearth where fire-irons hung below the open chimney. She sat beside the fire, her arms wrapped close about her chest, shivering with the cold, her face flushed.

"The boy . . . there's no one to care for him . . ." Her voice was faint and trembled.

The old women muttered together. "She's burning with fever!" Jessie observed. "Help me put her to bed."

" . . . no one to watch over him . . ." came the mother's plaintive cry, as the sisters took her from the fireside and helped her up the stairs.

Agatha placed her shawl around the sick woman's shoulders, and called back to the child: "Don't fret, little one. Your mother will be well again by and by. Wait there by the fire for a while."

He looked so lost and frightened standing there, watching them climb the stairs until they were out of sight. Emma watched them, too, and wondered at the old women's charity. They seemed so different now from the Devil Sisters whom she had seen lurking beside the grave in the cellar and pursuing her through the woods. Had they perhaps some sympathy with gipsies of which Emma was unaware?

A visitor herself in this forgotten place, and lost in the years gone by, she drew near to the boy – so close that she could read the fear in his eyes. He was no more than seven years old, and dressed in worn trousers and jersey, too threadbare to ward off the cold of winter.

It was only gradually that Emma began to recognise something strangely familiar about his expression – the sadness; his hair falling over his forehead in heavy locks; brown eyes fringed with long, dark lashes . . .

Emma blinked her eyes and peered closer still. There was no mistaking the features of the boy she had come upon in the attic room. Yet, by some vagary of time, he was now several years younger, and staring about the inside of a tavern he had never seen before.

"John!" she cried, reaching out to touch him. "It's Emma! Don't you remember me?"

His eyes were fixed on the stairway, with not even a flicker of recognition. It was not surprising that he should be unaware of her presence, she reflected sadly, for two or three summers had yet to pass before she came to visit the tavern. Once more time was weaving a tangled web, moving forward and backward in a pattern she could not understand.

"Often and often I have wondered about you," she was saying. But her voice drifted away, unheard, like the smoke wafting up the chimney.

Presently Jessie reappeared on the stairs, with words of comfort for the boy, and a hunk of bread and cheese for his supper. He sat in the hearth eating it greedily while Jessie watched him, casually brushing the locks from his eyes, or laying her hand on his shoulder.

"She's resting now," she told him. "Soon her fever will be gone and you can go on your way."

"Shall I see her?" asked the boy, his eyes misting with tears.

From the window Emma watched the snow drifts glisten in the last rays of sunshine. Dusk was falling, and shadows were stealing over the hills and woodland. Once again Tŷ-yn-y-Cysgodion had wrapped her in its spell: wrested her from a time measured on her grandfather's clocks and spirited her away to a winter long gone. She wondered when she would return to her own time, for whenever the house called her, each visit was longer than the last. On this occasion she feared she would wander alone, with no one to share her adventures.

"Come now, little gipsy boy," she heard Jessie say. "You must have a good night's sleep, and wake up fresh in the morning."

She took his hand and led him to the stairway in the corner. Emma followed them up the stairs and along the dusky corridor to a room where the boy's mother lay. Agatha was there, sitting beside the bed. The woman did not answer when the boy called to her. Her head moved restlessly on the pillow, and she whimpered as her fever raged.

Unwilling to leave, the boy clung to the bedclothes. But Jessie took him from the room, and back along the corridor; then up another flight of steps which led to the attic.

"You shall sleep here tonight," she told him. "Don't be afraid. We shall watch over your mother until she is well again."

When she had gone, the boy sat down on the bed, and in the fading light he looked around with some apprehension at the sloping walls and bare boards.

Emma was never far from his side. She strayed to the window to watch the twilight creep over the woods at Coed-y-Celyn; to the doorway to listen at the top of the stairs; and then back to the foot of the bed where she moved her hands before his eyes, and touched his cheek.

"John . . . John . . ." she was saying softly. "I will stay here for always. I won't leave you. Some day we will run away together – somewhere they will never find us!"

However she tried, she could not make her promise heard, nor dry his tears with her words of encouragement. They just kept trickling down his face as though he knew as surely as Emma that before long he would be alone, with no one in the world to watch over him.

CHAPTER 9

" . . . Time can never tear us apart . . ."

True to her promise, Emma stayed with the boy until darkness fell over the house, and he was fast asleep. For a long time she sat at the foot of his bed, wondering whether, on awakening, he would be aware of her presence, as he had one summer night when she first visited the attic room. Once in a while she stood beside him, leaning over to hear the sound of his breathing or a murmured cry as he stirred in his sleep. It was difficult to imagine the loneliness the boy would feel, for even when her own mother and father had gone there were always her grandparents to care for her. Soon he would have no one, save two old women who struck fear into Emma's heart and whom the boy had never known before.

As the hours passed she began to feel drowsy; and although she struggled to stay awake, at length she lay back, closed her eyes and allowed her thoughts to stray a hundred years away.

The moment she fell asleep, the spell was broken. For now, when she looked about her, there were clocks and ornaments still gleaming in the morning sunlight. The assortment of curios she had held in her arms had fallen to the floor; and her grandfather, startled by the clattering, came hurrying from the back room.

"What's happened?" he asked, noticing the expression of astonishment on Emma's face.

"I think I must have just . . . just stumbled for a moment," she faltered, blushing in her confusion. "There's nothing broken, as far as I can tell . . ." she went on defensively. And a voice in her thoughts whispered: "Nothing but the heart of a gipsy boy, who will now have no one to keep him company."

For the rest of the day Emma thought only of the boy she had forsaken in the attic room, and of his mother lying so ill, left to the mercy of the Devil Sisters. All the while she wondered why he seemed quite unaware of her presence there, when on other occasions – as an older boy – he had told of his troubles and begged her to stay. Perhaps now, while he was younger, he was not so lonely – not yet longing for company. Maybe in this phantom world, without substance or reality – where night and day and winter and summer described no regular pattern – maybe time was moving backwards, and her ghostly shape was growing faint.

Later that day, Emma wandered into the back room where, as usual, her grandfather was busy mending his clocks.

"Grandad . . ." she ventured, leaning across his bench and idly touching the wheels and springs littered around. "Grandad, is it possible that sometimes – in dreams perhaps – time could move backwards?"

"Only in fairy stories," her grandfather smiled. "Imagine what a crazy world that would be! Dark would follow the dawn, autumn would come before the summer, and old folk would be looking forward to their childhood! What's more," he teased with a feigned gasp of wonder, "in twelve years' time, my Beautiful Dreamer would be born!"

Emma's eyes brightened. "And as the years go rolling by," she said, "then that shadowy house beside the woods at Coed-y-Celyn would rise from the ruins, and all the people who are dead and gone would live there once again – just as they used to do!"

"Alas, time is like a river always flowing along. If only we could change its course," the old man sighed, stretching his aching back.

"Perhaps sometimes it changes just for a while," Emma persisted. "Not for always: not for ever and ever. During the quiet hours of the night perhaps, when we are sound asleep. Maybe then it steals backwards."

It was then that the clocks in the curiosity shop began to chime the hour, reminding the old man that time never falters – not even for a moment.

It was all quite bewildering. The way the paths of long ago became entangled with the present was a mystery that Emma would never understand. She wondered about it all evening long, and while she lay in bed that night.

There were many times during the spring and early summer when Emma went down into the cellar. But always it was quiet, and dark as night unless a candle was lit or the door above the stairs was left open to allow the daylight to come slanting down.

There was never a particular time when Emma was summoned to her world of make-believe – daytime or dark, when the moon was bright or the sky was overcast. There was no telling when she would be called. Often she had longed to return to discover a way by which she might lead the boy away from the clutches of the Devil Sisters, for she knew now that no harm would come to her. But it was never she who chose the time to come and go. She was not to know that one summer evening when she opened the door above the cellar stairs and descended into the dusky light, a further chapter in her adventures at Tŷ-yn-y-Cysgodion was about to begin.

Emma was near the bottom of the stairs when the door behind her closed, plunging the cellar into darkness. She turned at once, beginning to grope her way back along the banister rail. Then she became aware of furtive movement around her – a rustling sound barely perceptible, as though somehow the shape and contents of the cellar were changing. Suddenly she could no longer feel the rail, and feared she would fall over the edge of the stairs.

"Who's there?" someone called from the darkness below. "Who is it?"

Emma felt her heart beating fast, for she believed it was a voice she had heard before.

"John? . . ." she answered hesitantly. There was a further sound of movement – footsteps, she thought, coming towards her. "John . . . where are you?"

Gradually her eyes became accustomed to the dark, and a narrow rift of light beneath the door showed the black outlines of the walls and the shape of someone standing before her.

"Emma!" the voice cried; and now she was sure it was John hidden there in the dark – not beneath the stairs of the curiosity shop, but in that gloomy cellar under Tŷ-yn-y-Cysgodion where they had watched Evan Du and the Devil Sisters digging a grave for an ill-fated traveller.

"I searched for you all through the woods, and called to you, over and over," the boy went on; "but you were nowhere to be found. Then when it grew dark I lost my way . . ."

"Searched all through the woods?" Emma said in

81

bewilderment.

"I just ran on and on until I was too tired to go any farther," he continued. "Jessie and Agatha did not cross the stream, but no one can ever hide from them. All through the night the owls were crying and staring down at me . . ."

He fell silent for a while, and Emma heard him catch his breath as though he had been sobbing.

"At last I climbed into the low branches of a tree, where I could hide among the leaves. For hours I waited there. Then, when the daylight came, I heard someone coming, searching all round. It was Evan Du who came looking. Before long he was standing under the tree, looking up at me . . ."

Emma was remembering their escape from the tavern; their flight through the woods at Coed-y-Celyn; the sinister crows who hovered above them, circling the tree-tops, swooping low, pursuing, tormenting, until they reached a brook stretching across their path. She recalled the squawking of the birds – so like the raucous voice of Agatha calling after her.

"But that was long ago!" she told him. "Time is playing tricks with us – leaping from summer to winter and back again. Maybe for you it is moving forward, hour by hour, day by day; but for me it often flows in the opposite direction, back through the years. And sometimes, although the day wears on and the dusk turns to night, time stands still. If I were to stay here always I would never grow old. I should be a girl forever!"

The boy was silent again, wondering perhaps about the mysteries of time, or listening to the footsteps he heard approaching the door at the top of the stairs.

A moment later the key rattled in the lock and the door

opened. A shaft of daylight streamed into the cellar. The room where John was imprisoned was L-shaped, with bare walls and the floor crudely paved. In the corner, casks of ale were stacked one upon another.

The boy raised his hand to shield his eyes from the light, and then moved back into the darkness where he crouched against the wall as the heavy tread of Evan Du descended the stairs. Emma, too, retreated from his path, for he wore a fearful scowl as he approached them.

"Come on! There's work to be done, you mischievous Little Devil!" he growled. "Don't go hiding in the corner."

He seized the boy and dragged him from the wall, tearing at his jersey so roughly that he whimpered with fear. Plucking up her courage, Emma rushed to defend her companion, beating his assailant with her fists and crying out: "No! Don't hurt him! Leave him alone!" But her cries and struggles to free the boy from his clutches were as unavailing as a breath of wind.

Evan Du climbed the stairs, pulling the boy along behind him.

"If you wander off again," he warned, "you will be locked down in the cellar with the rats all day, and all night too!"

It was evening when Emma had been spirited away from the curiosity shop. Here, at the tavern, the sun was still high in the sky. It was the afternoon of some forgotten summer's day. The house was deserted, for it was usually dusk when travellers came for food and shelter for the night. There was no sign of the old women, and Emma imagined that they were out of sight in their room along the corridor upstairs, waiting for nightfall.

From the cellar the boy was taken across the cobbled yard to the stables, where he was put to work cleaning out

the stalls and filling the troughs with hay. Then there was
wood to be cut for the fire, mugs and plates to be scoured,
the tavern floor to be swept and covered with fresh straw
. . . His drudgery continued until he was weak with
exhaustion and the day was almost ended. And all the
while Evan Du was never far away, his cold eyes watching,
watching.

There was little Emma could do to help, except to raise
his hopes by telling of plans by which they might escape
from Tŷ-yn-y-Cysgodion. It was a promise she had made
more than once before. "We shall go after dark," she told
him again. "Then, while everyone is asleep, we can travel
so far away that no one will ever find us."

The boy looked at her reproachfully. "You promise to
stay; but when you're gone I shall be left alone. Before
long they will find my hiding-place and bring me back to
this place again."

"I never know when I shall come and go," Emma
protested. "Time has a magic that no one can understand.
It is like the darkness far, far beyond the sun – going on for
ever, with no beginning and no end."

John frowned, trying hard to understand what Emma
was saying. "Everyone knows that time just goes on and
on, from one day to the next," he said.

"Not always," Emma argued. "Sometimes it moves as
swiftly as a falling star, and other times it doesn't move at
all!"

"Time can never stand still!" John replied, raising his
voice. "Even when the clock stops, the sun is always
moving across the sky."

Emma pondered for a while, remembering how, in a
fleeting moment, seasons changed from winter to summer:
how, mysteriously, the boy had become young, and was

now older again.

"I believe I have found the secret," she said at last. "The time you know here at the tavern and the time measured on my grandfather's clocks have somehow become entangled. That's why things which happened long ago seem to have happened only yesterday."

She could see that still he did not understand.

"Why, the last time I came you were just a little gipsy boy, knocking on the door of the tavern. Do you remember how you stood there in the doorway, holding your mother's hand – afraid because she was so weak and burning with fever? The Devil Sisters – they were to watch over her; and you were left in the attic room. You were crying, and I was with you then, calling your name. But you didn't know I was there at all. Do you remember? . . ."

John had not forgotten his mother, for even now Emma could see his lips trembling and tears welling up in his eyes. She reminded him no more of those sad days.

"When everyone is asleep," she said, to drive away his tears, "we shall run off through the woods and far beyond; and whenever we stop to rest, we shall bind our wrists together with strong rushes. Then time can never tear us apart!"

Dusk was now falling, and they rested side by side on a bundle of hay in the stables. John was eating scraps of food he had stolen from the larder, while Emma laid plans for their escape and pondered on the mysteries of time.

Just then they heard footsteps approaching across the yard. When they looked around, they saw the figure of Evan Du framed in the doorway.

CHAPTER 10

". . . Open the door to no one! . . ."

The scarred-faced man looked at John suspiciously, and then his eyes wandered beyond him to the corners of the stable. He came close, grasping the boy's arm. Emma was there beside him, but he did not so much as glance in her direction.

"I heard a voice," he said gruffly. "Is somebody here?"

John shook his head. "There's no one," he answered, looking up into Evan Du's face and hiding a crust of bread behind his back. "You see, I'm all alone. There's no one here."

Evan Du pushed the boy aside while he searched among the stalls and behind the bundles of hay, several times moving past Emma as though she were no more than a shadow. "I heard someone," he kept muttering to himself. And when his foraging revealed no one hiding there he strode off across the yard towards the back door of the tavern.

Emma watched him until he disappeared into the dusky light beyond the doorway. "Why is he always so cruel?" she wondered, for she noticed how the boy trembled whenever he was near. "His eyes burn like fire!" she said with a shudder.

"He's cold-hearted and evil as the Devil himself!" John

whispered back.

The sky was darkening as they waited there together, for it was the boy's task to stable the horses of any travellers who rested for the night at the tavern. As the evening wore on, the sound of voices drifted through the open windows, and sometimes the swell of laughter from farmers who came to make merry after a long day in the fields. Once in a while the harsh voice of Evan Du would be raised above the others.

"Everyone fears his wicked temper and the sharp knife that hangs at his belt!" the boy warned. "There's no one who dares speak out against him."

Emma looked around at the gathering shadows in the stable. "Soon it will be dark and quiet when everyone is asleep," she said. "Then we can steal away and Evan Du and the Devil Sisters – they will never trouble you again."

She was remembering her last visit to Tŷ-yn-y-Cysgodion: when the leaves of time had flicked backwards to a far-gone winter's day, and a pale-faced gipsy boy, with his mother standing beside him, first came knocking at the door of the tavern.

"Long ago they took you in and cared for you," Emma recalled with a frown. "Don't you remember how you were cold and hungry? . . ." She hesitated for a moment, not wishing to bring back painful memories. "Your mother . . ." she went on cautiously, "even when she was so ill she thought only of you. They took you to her bedside – gave you food and shelter and spoke to you kindly . . . Why are they so cruel now?"

For a while John was silent, for he, too, was recalling the sadness of that winter day.

"I didn't see her ever again," he said at last. There were hardly any tears now. They were shed long ago, each night when he cried himself to sleep.

Emma learned how, on awakening in his attic room the next morning, Jessie had told him that his mother had become weaker during the night, and that now she had gone. "She is at peace now," the old woman had said. "But have no fear, we shall take care of you."

They had given him refuge, John recalled, but never sympathy or compassion. From dawn till dark he was made to work hard for his food and shelter; and whenever he tired they threatened to turn him out into the cold – to wander alone and sleep in the hills, for now, with his mother gone, he had no one who really cared for him.

"Then one evening, a long time afterwards, a seafaring man called at the tavern. He was dressed all in black, with a kerchief tied around his forehead and a scar across his cheek . . ."

"Evan Du!" Emma gasped.

"No one knows where he came from," the boy continued. "They said he had roamed the county, waylaying travellers on the highway. Others said that he was on his way to Ireland, seeking a berth at sea. But he had no horse, and only a few belongings carried in a bag over his shoulder, which he never let out of his sight."

But the black-hearted seafarer had abandoned his journey, it seemed, for night after night he was to be found drinking ale at the tavern, and consorting in secret with the sisters Agatha and Jessie.

"They were becoming too old and frail to carry on alone," John explained; "and not a soul hereabout would stay for long in such a gloomy house, with two strange old women to watch over them!"

As they sat there among the bundles of hay, remembering days gone by and reflecting on the dark deeds of Evan

Du, they hadn't noticed the moon grow brighter in the sky. They wandered to the stable doorway, where the lamplight in the tavern now spilled out across the cobbled yard, and the sound from within grew louder – the voice of Evan Du transcending all others.

"He has stayed here ever since," the boy concluded with a sigh, leading Emma to imagine how, at the bidding of the Devil Sisters, he struck fear into the hearts of ill-fated travellers who chanced to seek shelter for the night in the tavern somewhere in the woods at Coed-y-Celyn.

"When daylight comes," she promised again, "we shall be far away from here."

Yet John could not help but wonder where the ghost of a girl who rambled forward and backward in the realms of time, and through whose misty form even now the moon was shining – to what place could he follow her?

It was just then that their thoughts were disturbed by the clip-clopping of hooves on the cobble stones. A traveller was approaching the stables, leading his horse by the reins. A lantern fastened to the bridle was swinging to and fro and shone on the stranger's face. He wore a three-quarter length coat and a wide-brimmed hat. His step was weary, as though he had reached the end of a long journey. John went forward to meet him.

"Noswaith dda," (Good evening) he called with a jovial smile. "The old horse and I have travelled a long way and are thankful to find a place to rest."

The boy took the reins and led the horse into a stall where a trough of hay and a pail of water lay ready.

"Take good care of Poll," the traveller said, patting the mare affectionately. "She's tired and hungry, I shouldn't wonder." Then, after pressing a coin into the boy's hand for his trouble, he unhitched a satchel from the saddle and

89

made his way across the yard towards the back door of the tavern.

He was quite unaware of a girl who stood nearby, for the light from his lantern did not shine on her nor throw her shadow along the stable floor. Yet once, when she stretched out her hand to stroke the horse's mane, the animal reared its head restively, as though startled by some unnatural presence.

"Whoa there, Poll," John said softly. "There's no one here to harm you."

After a while the horse lowered its head to munch at the hay, and did not stir while Emma smoothed its neck and whispered in its ear. At length, when it was resting peacefully in the stall, they blew out the lantern and closed the stable door.

Many farmers in their coarse working clothes were gathered in the tavern, engaged in lively conversation. The boy passed among them on the way to his room in the attic; but no one bothered to glance at the companion who walked beside him. The traveller was sitting beside the fire with a mug of ale to settle the dust of the road.

Presently, when his mug was replenished, the traveller stood at the hearth and looked about the lamp-lit room. Then he raised his voice above the laughter and conversation, arresting everyone's attention.

"Brothers," he called to them. "I have journeyed all the way through Flint and Denbigh, and I have far to go."

His tone was deep and resonant, as though the scrubbed tables around the walls of the tavern were chapel pews and his fireside chair a pulpit. For a while the noise ceased. Mugs were lowered, and everyone fell silent, peering at him through the smoke-filled room.

"I come to you as a servant of the Lord, to spread His

gospel and build His house among you. Spare a little of what you have, and many times you shall be rewarded."

The preacher passed among them, holding out his satchel already laden with alms. There was a jingle of coins as coppers were dropped in to swell his collection. He blessed each one who contributed, plunging his hand deep into the satchel: proud to display the silver, gold and copper coins donated to the house of God by folk of the northern towns and hamlets. He blessed them all – even those who scowled and turned away.

"Rich shall be your reward!" he told them again. And before retiring he let it be known that the following morning at first light he would be journeying on through Betws-y-Coed to the good folk of Caernarfon. Then, with his satchel of alms slung over his shoulder, he made his way up the stairs to a room along the corridor. As he went off to bed the tavern was once again alive with merriment.

It had not escaped John's attention that from behind the counter upon which the casks of ale stood, Evan Du, his eyes smouldering with greed, watched the preacher until he disappeared into the darkness.

"Look!" the boy said, pointing towards the blackguard, and then Emma, too, could sense the mischief stirring in Black Evan's thoughts.

They followed the preacher up the stairs and along to a room at the end of the corridor. There they listened at the door, while inside the weary traveller prepared to settle down to his night's rest.

"They'll wait until the house is quiet," John whispered. "Then when he's asleep they'll open the door . . ."

"We must warn him!" Emma urged; for already she had fearful visions of a shallow grave dug in the cellar floor. "They wouldn't . . . murder him!" she trembled.

91

"His satchel is filled with money," the boy answered grimly; "and he's travelling all alone."

First he peered back along the corridor for fear he should see the silhouette of Evan Du appear at the top of the stairs. Then he knocked quietly on the door.

The preacher was surprised to find the boy from the stable standing there in the doorway. He held a candle close, but it was only John's shadow that darkened the wall.

"Well now, young man," he inquired with a smile. "What brings you knocking at old Josiah's door? Nothing ailing Old Poll, I trust?" he added with some anxiety.

The boy hesitated. "No . . . No, sir. She's resting peacefully enough in her stall," he said. But he was wondering, he went on to explain, whether the preacher would remember to be on his guard and bolt the door before going to sleep, for there were times when the tavern harboured covetous thieves who might steal into his room in the quiet of night. "Take care, sir," he warned. "Open the door to no one! You wouldn't believe how cunning they can be!"

Old Josiah thanked him kindly for his concern and begged him have no fear. "For the Lord will watch over His servants and keep them safe from the mischief of the Devil!" he muttered as though in silent prayer.

Then he bade the boy goodnight and closed the door, remembering to fasten the bolt against any intruder who might be lurking in the night.

They made their way back along the corridor towards the flight of stairs leading to the attic; and as they passed the room occupied by the sisters Jessie and Agatha, they noticed a light glowing beneath the door, and heard a muttering of voices coming from inside.

When they had hurried past, John whispered: "Sometimes I wonder if they sleep by day and keep watch through the night like the owls in the wood."

From the window in the attic room Emma gazed over the hills in the distance with the moonlight shining on them, and the wooded valleys shrouded with darkness. She longed to return to her own time – to her room above the curiosity shop overlooking the streets, where pools of light glimmered under the gas lamps – and for John to be there beside her.

CHAPTER 11

". . . Who's there? . . ."

The time passed slowly as they waited in the attic room, looking out over the hills, listening to the swell of voices rising from downstairs. At length they saw the local farmers leaving the tavern and trudging home along the path below the window.

The house became silent – almost as though it, too, were listening . . . listening.

Tired after an eventful day and having had little rest the night before, John sometimes lay on the bed and closed his eyes. But he fought against a longing to sleep, fearing that when he awoke Emma would be gone. It was her presence in the room and occasionally the sound of her voice that kept him awake.

"Soon they will all be asleep," she reminded him. "Then we can set off on our journey with the moonlight to guide us."

"We shall never escape from them," John replied despondently, believing that the Devil Sisters would soar into the sky like witches on broomsticks, searching the woods and glades with eyes like hawks.

"We will go into the hills," Emma decided, "travelling while it's dark and hiding in caves by day. We shall go so far they could never . . ."

Her voice trailed away when she noticed that once again the boy's eyes were closed and he was lying quite still.

He looked so peaceful lying there in the candlelight, his hair tumbled, shadows about his eyelids, and cheeks as pale as the pillow upon which he lay. Emma hadn't the heart to disturb him. It hadn't occurred to her that although it was now late at night she didn't feel tired herself.

While the boy slept she went to listen at the door, and then ventured down the stairs and along the corridor. It was dimly lit by the moonlight that filtered through the window at the far end, and the only sound was the murmur of voices coming from the Devil Sisters' room where the glow of lamplight still showed beneath the door.

Then there came another sound that startled her. Footsteps were coming up the stairs from the tavern. Looking over her shoulder, Emma saw the silhouette of Evan Du moving towards her. She pressed herself against the wall as he approached; and he passed so close to her that she heard the sound of his breathing. A moment later he was listening at the door of the old women's room.

Agatha came to answer his knocking, and presently Jessie joined them in the doorway. For some time they whispered together secretly, and although Emma couldn't hear what they were saying, she suspected that they were talking about Old Josiah, the preacher who was travelling from county to county collecting alms for the Church, for Evan Du was pointing towards his room at the end of the corridor. Emma stifled a cry of horror when he unsheathed the knife that hung at his belt and crept to the preacher's door!

Quietly he turned the handle, but the door would not open. Once more he tried, leaning against it with his shoulder, but still the bolt held fast.

95

"Who's there?" the preacher called from inside.

Evan Du did not answer him. He was hiding in the shadows, waiting for the door to open.

"What do you want?" the voice called again. "If you're a servant of the Devil, beware the wrath of the Lord – and the pistol I hold ready in my hand!"

In the silence that followed, the Devil Sisters beckoned to Evan Du, and he gave up his attempt to lure the preacher out into the corridor. Replacing the knife in its sheath, he returned to their doorway.

"He's too cunning for you," Emma heard them whisper. "But never fear, it's a long time before sunrise." Then their shoulders rocked with quiet laughter, as though they were hatching some fiendish plot.

The lamplight in their room shone out through the open door and fell upon Emma. But no one saw her standing there. Not even the Devil Sisters were aware of her presence.

There was more murmuring and furtive glances towards the door of their overnight lodger before Evan Du went off into the darkness downstairs, and the old women returned to their room, closing the door behind them.

While John was asleep in the attic it was left to Emma to keep watch on the Devil Sisters: to wait until their room was in darkness and the house was still; for only then would it be safe for them to make their escape.

As the night wore on she roamed the house, moving along the stairs and passages with never a creak from the boards upon which she trod. And for a long time no sound came from within the rooms she passed. Wherever the moonlight shone through the windows thunderous shadows gathered all about, some shaped like outstretched arms waiting to embrace her. At every turn and alcove she was half-afraid she would encounter a tall man, black as the shadows. But in her wandering she found no sign of Evan Du.

"Perhaps he's down in the cellar," she whispered to herself, "digging a grave to hide the body of Old Josiah! But there," she argued, "even if I were to stand beside him and scream 'Thief! . . . Murderer!' he would see only his own shadow, and hear only the faint squealing of rats as they scampered about. After all, *I* should be almost a hundred years away!"

Upstairs and downstairs she wandered, but whenever she passed the door half-way along the corridor a thin shaft of light was spilling from the room. Emma began to wonder whether Jessie and Agatha slept while the lamp was burning; but once in a while she heard the murmur of their voices. Perhaps what John had said was true – that they slept by day and kept watch through the night like the owls in the wood.

Her vigil continued for a long time. She hadn't come upon Evan Du lurking about in the corridor, nor had the Devil Sisters opened their door. Yet, as midnight passed, a fearful noise coming from within Old Josiah's room made her tremble with fright and hurry up the flight of stairs to the attic . . .

When he was confident that the intruder at his door had been frightened away, the preacher had gone back to sleep. However, shortly after midnight he woke again when he felt a movement on and around his feet. The blanket stirred, and he heard a scratching sound at the bottom of the bed. He sat up, listening. The disturbance came again – this time the sound of quiet steps, scuffling around the floor.

His voice trembled. "Who's there?"

All was quiet for a while. Then the soft padding of footfalls continued, and he was aware of some creature – some *thing* – jumping on and off the bedclothes, pulling at them.

Old Josiah was numbed with fright. He could see nothing through the darkness, but was conscious of furtive movement about him. When it ceased for a few moments he fumbled at the bedside and lit a candle.

Peering into the corners of the room he saw no one, but knew that something was lurking in the shadows – watching him! He whispered a prayer that he be protected from the mischief of the Devil, and held the satchel tightly in his arms. Then as silence prevailed, he got out of bed and began to search around.

The door and window remained closed and securely fastened. His clothes were strewn about the floor, and the blanket was dishevelled. The room was sparsely furnished – the bed, with a small, rickety table beside it upon which the candlestick stood, a chair, and an old wardrobe against the wall.

"Who's there?" Old Josiah whispered again.

No one answered him.

Then, when he looked up, he was startled to see two pairs of eyes glowing as brightly as the candle flame, staring at him. There was a sudden animal cry and two black cats leapt down. With arched backs and bristled fur, they slunk about, spitting and growling. Then they bared their teeth and sprang toward him, tearing at his sleeve with needle-like claws, piercing his flesh as he raised his arm to ward them off. They leapt and scratched with intense ferocity, attacking from every direction. He flung one from his shoulder, crying out in pain as it bit at his throat.

During his struggle to keep the fearful creatures at bay, the chair was overturned, and the force of their onslaught threw him to the floor. The preacher lurched and kicked and, grasping a fire-iron from the grate, struck out wildly. One of the cats let out a piercing cry and then, together, both animals scampered into the darkness of the fireplace.

It was some time before Old Josiah regained some measure of composure. He put a match to the kindling lying in the grate and watched the smoke and flames lick the chimney. But the cats had vanished ...

The boy was still asleep when Emma reached the attic room.

"John ... John!" she whispered, shaking his shoulder to awaken him.

Startled, he sat up, staring about the room as though he had wakened from a nightmare.

"Old Josiah –" Emma said, "someone's in his room! There was a fearful noise, and I heard his voice crying out!"

They crept down to the corridor and listened from the bottom of the stairs. A light still shone under the door of the old women's room, but there was no sound. They waited there, peering into the dusky light that filtered in through the far window, and into the darkness above the stairway leading down to the tavern. But the house was silent as a tomb.

"It sounded as though he were struggling for his life," Emma murmured, her eyes fixed on the black outline of the traveller's door. "Cries of fright and furniture falling to the floor ..."

But the boy's gaze was drawn elsewhere – to a light showing beneath another doorway.

"Sometimes I wonder if they ever sleep," he said absently. "All through the night their lamp is burning."

The darkness had worn on, and before long the first light of dawn would appear. The plight of Old Josiah and the mischievous schemes of Evan Du and the Devil Sisters had driven from Emma's thoughts all their plans to run away into the hills: to set off with the moonlight to guide them while everyone was asleep. Now their chance had gone, and John began to despair of ever escaping from his sinister guardians and his misery at Tŷ-yn-y-Cysgodion.

"I shall never be free," he said ruefully. "Not until Agatha and Jessie lie buried in the churchyard!"

Emma didn't notice the sadness in his voice. Her mind was filled with thoughts of Old Josiah – with visions of his body lying crumpled on the floor of his room, of a fresh grave being dug in the cellar.

"If Old Josiah . . . If he is never seen again," she faltered, "what will become of Poll?"

She imagined the preacher's faithful mare being driven from the stable to fend for herself, searching among the hills for a master who would never be found. And now Emma was sad too.

It was then that a sudden notion leapt into the boy's thoughts, and his eyes brightened with excitement. "If Old Josiah is never seen again," he said, "then we could take the horse and gallop away so fast and far that no one would ever catch us!"

There was still no sound to disturb the silence: no stealthy figures moving along the corridor. They retraced their steps, and from the attic window watched for the first light of dawn to show above the hills.

After a while they both fell silent, wrapped in their own thoughts. Emma was wondering how much longer she was destined to stay in this world of long ago, where days and nights passed by in less than a fleeting moment of her own time.

John had visions of rushing along through the valleys and over the hills, high in the saddle of Poll, with the faint figure of a girl sitting behind him, her arms about his waist, her fair hair blowing in the wind.

CHAPTER 12

". . . He'll never give up . . ."

Old Josiah heard no further sound that night. When the kindling had smouldered to ashes in the grate he kept watch in the candlelight of his room, constantly glancing into the corners, listening for the slightest rustle. But the cats, with their wild eyes and bristled fur, had vanished. Although he searched every nook and cranny, there was no sign of them. Even when he poked into the darkness of the chimney with the fire-iron, not a whimper did he hear. The intruders had gone as mysteriously as they had appeared.

Now, clothed in his three-quarter length coat and wide-brimmed hat, Old Josiah sat on the edge of the bed, clutching his satchel and waiting for daylight to come.

John's work began early each morning. Whenever travellers broke their journey for a night's rest at the tavern it was his task to feed and saddle their horses, or hitch them to the carriage, ready for a fresh start.

That morning, as he fed and groomed Poll, Emma watched anxiously from the stable door for the preacher to appear.

"I'm thinking his journey will end here," John remarked grimly. "'He's lost his way or been set upon by some highway robber' – that's what everyone will say. That's what they always say when travellers are never seen again."

Emma shuddered with horror.

"Old Josiah had a pistol!" she remembered. "I heard him call out when Evan Du was at his door. He wouldn't dare . . ."

Her voice broke off suddenly when she saw the door at the rear of the tavern open and a gentleman in a wide-brimmed hat emerge.

"It's Old Josiah!" she cried, breathing a sigh of relief. "It's the preacher – safe and sound!"

As he drew close Emma noticed his eyes rimmed red from lack of sleep. The side of his face was scratched, and he wore the expression of someone frightened and bewildered. He came into the stable, passing right through Emma, who was standing in the doorway, as though she were just a pale ray of morning sunshine.

"There are dark spirits abroad in this ungodly house!" he muttered, more to himself than to the boy fastening the saddle on his chestnut mare. Then, raising his voice: "Bless you, my son, for your timely warning last night. I do believe the Devil himself is up to his mischief hereabouts. I'll be glad to turn my back on this evil place!"

For a while John was silent. Then, as he led Poll from the stall, he looked beyond the preacher toward the back door of the tavern, fearing that Evan Du would appear there.

"It's Jessie and Agatha," the boy began. "Two old women with their witching spells! Hidden away in their room, with the curtains always closed to shut out the daylight, and a blazing fire in the grate come winter or summer . . . with withered plants and nightshade berries and all manner of dead creatures lying about the hearth! No one would believe how wicked and cunning they can be!"

The preacher took the reins and fastened his satchel to the saddle.

"And there's black-hearted Evan," John went on, glancing all round. "Evan Du they call him. He was always a thief – and a murderer, too, if the truth were known!"

"Last night he came to your door with his dagger drawn!" Emma called from the doorway. But Old Josiah could not hear her voice. He heard only the distant trill of a skylark hovering over the woodland.

The preacher turned to the boy with a worried frown. "They're not your kin?" he asked incredulously.

"No, sir," John replied sadly. "I'm all alone. There's only . . ."

He pointed towards the doorway, where Emma, his only friend, was standing like a swirl of morning mist. Then he remembered that she was only a ghost whom no one else could see.

"There's only my mother, and now she's gone . . ."

"She died of a fever long ago, and the Devil Sisters kept him here," Emma explained. But, to the preacher, her voice was almost a hundred years away.

"Have you nowhere to go – no other kinfolk of your own?" Old Josiah asked.

John lowered his head. "Sometimes I run away," he said. "But I can never hide from Jessie and Agatha. Before nightfall Evan Du comes to drag me back again. Then I'm beaten and locked in the cellar, cold and hungry."

Old Josiah was filled with dismay. "If they're so cruel and care nothing for you, why should they want you to stay?" he wondered.

Once again John glanced all about, fearing someone else might be listening. "They're afraid of what I've seen and heard – afraid I should tell," he replied.

"Perhaps Old Josiah will take us with him," Emma urged. "He's travelling far off to the mountains of Caernarfon. No one would follow us there!"

The preacher was looking at John's pale cheeks and deep brown eyes that seemed too large for his face; at the ragged clothes of a child whom clearly no one cared for.

"Then you're all alone in the world," he said with a kindly smile.

John nodded. "Please, sir . . ." he ventured. "I was wondering . . . if you are going on a journey far away, I was wondering if we . . . *I* might come with you? . . ."

The preacher hesitated, looking again at the boy's frail limbs and appealing eyes.

"I'll be no trouble," John hastened to assure him. "Somewhere I will find a gipsy camp where I could stay. They are the only folk I understand. Here I am just a prisoner, working hard from dawn till nightfall with hardly an hour to rest."

"They'll never let him wander far," Emma sighed. "They'll weave some spell to capture him."

"I can take care of Poll," the boy went on, "and help watch out for thieves as we travel along the lonely roads."

When Old Josiah led his mare out into the cobbled yard and climbed into the saddle, the sunlight was already shining through the trees.

"Come along," he said, stretching out his hand to help John scramble up beside him. "This is no place for an orphan boy. The Devil himself abides in this bleak house! You can travel with me to the good folk of Caernarfon."

Emma, too, climbed up behind them, with little difficulty and no extra burden for Poll, for the ghost of years to come had no weight at all.

With a flick of the reins they set off on their journey to the west, turning for a last, lingering glance at Tŷ-yn-y-Cysgodion. It was then they saw the back door of the tavern opening wide; and there, framed in the doorway, stood Agatha leaning on her stick, and beside her the gaunt figure of Jessie.

Old Josiah was staring at them, recalling the fearful happenings of the night – the steathly movement about his bed, two pairs of eyes burning in the darkness, his striking out with the fire-iron at the wild creatures that attacked him. He began to wonder at their witchcraft, for he could see that Jessie's arm, hanging limply at her side, was swathed in bandage – red with blood from a recent wound!

The Devil Sisters didn't call after them. As they watched the preacher and the boy riding away they chuckled together and murmured one with the other as though they shared a secret.

"They know which road he's travelling along," Emma whispered to John. "Perhaps Evan Du is hiding somewhere, waiting for us to pass by."

The road stretched before them, winding its way over the side of a hill and down into a valley. Once in a while Emma would look back over her shoulder and watch the grey walls of Tŷ-yn-y-Cysgodion and the trees which held the house in their shadow slip farther and farther away. Wistfully she wondered if somewhere beyond the horizon they would come upon a different time and a distant town where familiar streets would lead them to her grandfather's curiosity shop.

They rode on in silence, each wrapped in thought. Old Josiah was reliving the nightmare that had kept him from his sleep: the mystery, the moments of terror. John was thankful for every step that took him farther from his days of misery and loneliness. In some glade they were sure to find a gipsy band gathered about their caravans. He would be welcome among them: welcome to share their life of roaming the hills, sleeping under the stars. And when Emma's thoughts had dwelt for a while on the perplexity of time and its crazy boundaries, she listened to the sheep bleating on the hillside and the monotonous rhythm of the horse's hooves as they trotted along the road.

Whenever they passed a clump of trees, or the road was lined with hedges, Emma and John kept watch for a scarred-faced man dressed all in black who might be lurking at the roadside.

"If he's lying in wait," Emma whispered, "he'll spring upon us suddenly."

She pointed to the satchel, bulging with coins, which hung beside them. "He's afraid Old Josiah has a pistol!"

Before the road descended into the valley John and the preacher dismounted to give Poll a rest. They walked beside the mare while Emma remained in the saddle, for her weight was no burden at all. And it was Emma, from her vantage point, who first saw a movement in a copse ahead of them and caught sight of Evan Du hiding there, waiting for them.

No sooner had John heard her warning cry than their assailant was upon them, springing from the seclusion of trees and seizing the reins. Startled, the mare reared and broke free, galloping off along the hillside with Emma clinging on. John, too, fled in terror when he saw the glint of the blackguard's knife.

It was some time before he looked back to see Old Josiah lying beside the road, with Evan Du bending over him.

"Thief! . . . Murderer!" he cried, his heart pounding, his voice trembling with fear and anger.

He dared not to go to the preacher's aid, for Evan Du's face was twisted with rage; and even had he the courage, he feared it was too late to help him now, because Old Josiah lay still and made no sound. Their assailant left the body sprawled on the ground and gave chase, overtaking the boy with every stride.

John ran towards the horse, with Evan Du in close pursuit. Emma cried out as her companion approached, urging him to run faster, faster. And the sound of her voice echoed across the valley.

Their attacker was almost upon them when the boy managed to scramble up into the saddle beside her, and they spurred the mare into a gallop, leaving Evan Du to shake his fists and hurl threats after them.

Along the road down into the valley they went, as fast as Old Poll would carry them, John riding skilfully and Emma's arms wound tightly around his waist. They didn't stop until the old mare was panting with exhaustion and their pursuer was left far behind.

"He'll never give up," John sighed as they rested beside a brook. "He daren't let me escape to tell what I know. If the magistrates should learn of their wickedness they will all end their days hanging from the gallows!"

Emma looked back. The road appeared to be deserted, but she knew that somewhere Evan Du was following their trail or cutting across the valley to lie in wait where the road swung around to climb the shoulder of the hill on the opposite side. Reflecting on their last endeavour to escape the clutches of the Devil Sisters – their flight through the woods at Coed-y-Celyn – Emma's eyes searched the sky, afraid she would see two black crows hovering there, waiting to swoop upon them with a squawking and a flurry of feathers. But she heard only the song of a skylark, hidden in the glare of the morning sun.

"Old Josiah . . ." Emma began. "We can't leave him!"

John lowered his head, avoiding her gaze. "We can't help him now," he said, for he remembered the glint of Evan Du's dagger and had seen how still the preacher lay on the ground. "No one can help him now."

Before long they were on their way again, following the road through the valley, pausing at frequent intervals to look behind or to scan the hillside all around.

When they came to the horseshoe bend they left the road and headed north, afraid that Evan Du would waylay them. They clambered up the hill, leading the mare by the reins and urging her forward as she struggled to keep her footing on the grassy slopes. Upward and onward they trudged on their journey, climbing into the saddle when the path before them was firm and level, always wary of their black-hearted pursuer whom they feared might be lurking behind every rock and bank of ferns.

"He'll never give up," John said again, for in his heart he knew that if he were allowed to escape, to tell of the grisly deeds he had witnessed – of ill-fated travellers, robbed of their valuables, whose bodies now lay buried in the cellar – then Evan Du and the witches of Tŷ-yn-y-Cysgodion would surely be sought and pay for their wickedness with their lives.

"Would he . . . would he murder you, too?" Emma shuddered, her eyes wide with horror.

John looked at her ruefully. "He would kill me in an instant if he thought I would escape to tell of his wickedness. In the tavern he watches me like a hawk and lets me speak to no one." Fear showed in his eyes. "Many times he has sworn to cut out my tongue if I breathe a word!"

Emma gasped and quickly turned to look over her shoulder.

"Besides," the boy went on, "if I were gone then there would be no one to tend the horses and clean out the stables and slave from morning till night. And there's not another soul who would stay at the tavern once the shutters are closed – no one save for weary travellers who come from far away. They don't know what danger awaits them there."

"Perhaps Agatha and Jessie have promised always to give you shelter," Emma suggested. She wondered for a moment whether they had found any pity in their hearts for an orphan.

"Their hearts are as hard as flint," John answered. He was sure they would shelter him only so long as they had use for him, and so long as their dark deeds were kept secret.

In his imagination John saw Evan Du springing from a hiding place beside their path. He saw his lips twist cruelly, his knife drawn from its sheath. It was then that he remembered Old Josiah's pistol. He leaned down, opening the satchel that hung from the saddle. He fumbled among the coins, but found no pistol hidden there.

More than an hour passed before they stopped to rest again. During that time they had urged Poll into a gallop once they had reached the crest of the hill and the path before them was clear. On and on they had raced, mile after mile, until the poor mare was near exhaustion. They were sure now that no matter how fast their pursuer ran he could never catch up with them. Only then did they dare to rest.

While Poll lowered her head to graze in the shade of a copse, John and Emma lay in the heather, looking up into the sky, for they knew that Evan Du was left far behind. They were not to know that he had found their trail, and had not given up the chase.

"The shadowy house will never be the same without you," Emma said sadly. "If ever I go there again it will be a place of fear and darkness, with only travellers from long ago, Evan Du and the Devil Sisters wandering the stairs and corridors . . ."

As they lay there talking together they had, for a while, forgotten their pursuer who was scrambling up the shoulder of the hill and nearing the crest.

"Among them I shall be all alone," Emma went on. "No one would glance at a girl from some other time. I should just pass through the shadows as ghosts are said to do."

"Somewhere, some time, we shall meet again," the boy told her. "Maybe on the other side of the mountains we shall find a strange, new world – that Otherworld where streets are lined with lamplight and buildings stand side by side. Perhaps we shall come upon the time where you belong – even that old curiosity shop where you live with your grandfather and grandmother. Wouldn't that be wonderful!"

They talked of Emma's world and the Otherworld of Tŷ-yn-y-Cysgodion, and of a place beyond the mountains where past and future may some day come together.

Time was passing, faster than they realised. Had they known that a figure dressed all in black was now approaching the copse where they rested, they would have fled farther into the hills. Poll raised her head and pricked up her ears, but neither John nor Emma heard the distant footfalls. They lay there a little while longer.

"It's strange that they never miss me while I'm away," Emma said mysteriously. "However long I stay – hours or even days – it seems that time stands still. Not a moment of my wandering is measured on my grandfather's clocks. Gran says they're just daydreams : make-believe journeys – all visions of my imagination. Sometimes I wonder if what she says is true."

"Maybe . . ." said John, rising from the heather and clicking his tongue to call the mare from her grazing, "maybe when you are home again you should turn back the hands of the clock over and over. Then I could be there with you. Together we could . . ."

The swiftness and cunning of Black Evan's pursuit had taken them by surprise. Now he was upon them, his figure emerging from behind a tree trunk, dark and menacing. They were frozen with terror as he stood there glaring at John with burning eyes.

"Gipsy devil!" he snarled, seizing the boy and holding him fast. "I should cut your heart out for carrying mischievous tales to strangers!"

He did not hear Emma's piercing scream go echoing through the valley; and her desperate struggle to wrest her companion from the villain's grasp was of no avail. He beat the boy mercilessly, until his face was bruised and bleeding and he lay senseless on the ground. Then he bound his hands with the kerchief he wore about his neck and threw him across the horse's back so that his hands and feet hung down on either side.

"If I have my way," he threatened with a grimace, "your secrets will be buried with you in the cellar!"

Then began their journey back to the tavern, Evan Du remorseless in the saddle, his prisoner quite still. And Emma, with a dread foreboding of the fate that awaited the boy, striving to keep up with them, all the while calling: "Don't be afraid. I'll not leave you, John. I will never leave you again!"

CHAPTER 13

". . . Will I be coming back again? . . ."

Before the morning was over, the ivy-clad walls of Tŷ-yn-y-Cysgodion appeared on the horizon, and soon Emma found herself following Evan Du and his captive along the path through the trees that led to the tavern.

From an upstairs window Agatha and Jessie were peering down at them, grinning with satisfaction now that the boy had been recaptured; and likely thankful that the preacher with whom he had escaped now lay somewhere at the roadside, unable to carry tales of their mischief.

By this time John had regained consciousness. In a last desperate effort, he kicked and writhed and called out for help. But with the over-powering grasp of Evan Du to hold him fast his struggles were in vain.

"Gipsy devil!" Evan Du growled again. "You will stay here where you belong. I shall be watching, like a hawk watches a sparrow!"

"I'd rather be dead and buried in the cellar!" the boy cried defiantly, and winced with pain as his captor's grasp tightened. Then he heard Emma's voice calling, urging him not to despair.

"Don't be afraid, John," she said. "They can't keep you here forever!"

When they approached the tavern door Evan Du

dismounted, pulling the boy from Poll's back and unhitching the satchel from the saddle. He then drove the mare away, pelting her with stones to frighten her off into the woodland. He was careful to leave no trace of Old Josiah's visit the previous night. When the preacher's body was discovered lying beside the road and his horse found straying through the woods at Coed-y-Celyn, some other highway robber would be blamed.

Muttering oaths and threatening to silence the boy for ever, Evan Du then forced him indoors, dragging him along a passage-way and down over the steps leading to the cellar, pressing his hand over his mouth to stifle his cries. There he was thrown to the floor; and no sooner had Emma followed him inside than the door slammed behind them, leaving the prisoners together. Evan Du's footsteps were heard moving away. Then for a time all was silent.

The chink of light that showed beneath the door was too dim to brighten the darkness so Emma had to feel her way along the wall.

"John," she whispered. "John, where are you?"

No one answered her. There was no sound – not even the faint screeching of rats scurrying around the floor. She feared that when he was hurled into the cellar he had struck his head against the wall and now lay unconscious again in the corner.

"If only I could untie your hands! John . . . where are you?"

The silence continued. Then it seemed that in the darkness of the cellar there appeared a darker cavern, receding into the distance like a black whirlpool, drawing her into its depths, closing in all round her. Farther and deeper it swirled her away, her thoughts reeling, her cry of alarm echoing.

When, at last, all was still, Emma became aware of furtive movement about her; and faint inanimate sounds, as though the contents of the cellar were drifting away and different objects were taking their place.

She groped her way towards the light shining under the door, and fumbled for the latch. To her surprise the door was unlocked, and when she opened it wide the light flooded in. Behind her there was no L-shaped room with bare walls and a paved floor: no casks of ale stacked in the corner. Instead, the cellar was strewn with old curios and picture frames all grey with dust. Once more time had leapt a hundred summers, leaving the boy imprisoned beneath the tavern to the years long gone, and spiriting Emma back to the cellar of her grandfather's curiosity shop. "Why, Emma, you're as pale as a ghost!"

Emma's grandfather had finished tinkering with his clocks in the back room when she reappeared after her visit to the cellar and closed the door above the stairs. Now he was looking at his granddaughter anxiously. "What's troubling you, my love?" he frowned.

For a while Emma just stood there in a daze. Then she sighed, not knowing how to answer him. How could *anyone* believe that her adventures through daytime and dusk and hours of darkness should unfold in only a fleeting moment? Who could imagine that Otherworld where time was inconstant and changed as swiftly as the pattern of clouds on a windy day?

"While I was in the cellar the door closed behind me," she replied hesitantly. "Perhaps it was the sudden darkness that startled me."

Together they fastened the shutters over the window of the curiosity shop and made their way upstairs, where Emma's grandmother was preparing their supper.

For the rest of the evening Emma was quiet, thinking only of that long-forgotten place set back among the trees at the roadside. It seemed that each journey she made was longer than the one before. Maybe when next she wandered there some infinite moment would keep her forever imprisoned in the past.

She was remembering all that had happened during her last visit to Tŷ-yn-y-Cysgodion – the arrival of Old Josiah, weary after his pilgrimage through the northern counties; a night of watching and waiting, listening for sounds in the dark; their flight to the hills, pursued by Evan Du; the preacher lying still at the roadside . . .

"When the cellar door closed and I was left there in the darkness . . ." Emma began, while her grandmother was busy in the kitchen and couldn't overhear what she was saying. "While I was away, did you think I had fallen asleep? Were you searching for me everywhere? I was missing for such a long time!"

Her grandfather looked surprised. "Why, you were alone hardly any time at all," he explained. "No longer than it takes to walk down the steps and back again."

Once more Emma wondered at the mysteries of time. It was true, she thought, that the hours spent in her phantom world were stolen hours which passed unmeasured, unnoticed by anyone else. Often and often it tormented her that no one would listen – no one would ever understand . . .

The days of summer passed by and lengthened into weeks. Never once did she mention the house in the shadows; but not a day went by without her wondering . . . remembering: recalling her fear of two old women who stole about at night to weave their mischief and awesome spells; her

117

horror of a black-hearted seafarer and his murderous deeds; of Poll, roaming the hills in search of a master whom she would never find again. In her thoughts, and sometimes in her dreams, Emma remembered them all. And John – with sadness her thoughts dwelt on him more often than on all the others. Once in a while she was tempted to steal down to the cellar and stare into the picture of the tavern; or to close the door behind her and wait there in the darkness. Perhaps then she would be spirited away to the cellar of Tŷ-yn-y-Cysgodion, where her companion of long ago would be lying in the corner, longing to hear her voice.

But then, she wondered, would the years have leapt backward or forward? Would she find that John had grown older or had become a young boy again and not notice her at all? There was no accounting for the strange patterns that time might weave.

"What if I should be imprisoned there, never to return again!" she would whisper to herself, and then stop at the door leading to the cellar, afraid to venture down the stairs.

And so, whether she were at home or at school, Emma was left to wonder alone about past journeys to a fearful house that had long since fallen to ruin. She had only to mention the House in the Shadows to bring the sighs of reproach from her grandmother. And when once at school she told of her friend in some Otherworld: of an orphan, bound and held captive by two witches and a scarred-faced rogue . . . when she told of such a place the children who listened laughed derisorily.

"You will *never* understand!" Emma countered fiercely. And the more earnestly she declared that her story was true the longer became their taunting. It seemed that no one would ever share the secret of her journeys into the past. Then one evening later that summer she was encouraged to believe that this would not always be so . . . .

It was the time when a travelling fair had come to town, and folk went flocking to the market square, attracted by the sounds of music and hawkers calling. His day's work over, old Mr Dalamore decided to put up the shutters earlier than usual and to take his granddaughter along to watch the festivity.

"It might put the sparkle back in her eyes," Emma's grandmother agreed. "She's been so unhappy these past weeks – always so quiet, and wearing that far-away look. Goodness knows what's troubling her. 'It's only my day-dreams,' she says whenever I ask. Perhaps the fun at the fair will cheer her up." She would have liked to accompany them, she sighed; but it would be so crowded and noisy there. Instead she would stay at home and prepare supper.

In the twilight, Emma and her grandfather made their way toward the market square. Before long they were among the crowds of people and the sounds of a thousand murmuring voices. Vendors called to passers-by from behind their stalls. Some were heaped with fresh fruit, others arrayed with glittering trinkets or jars of sweets or rolls of bright material. There were roundabouts and hoop-la and a coconut shy, bringing cries of excitement. But Emma glanced at these with hardly a glimmer of interest. It seemed strange that strolling among a throng of people she should feel so alone. Nothing she saw brought a smile to her face. Even in the gallery of mirrors where grotesque reflections moved all about them she didn't laugh with the others. Instead she imagined that she saw the bent figure of Agatha, the gaunt image of Jessie, or that the face of Evan Du was leering back at her.

Of all the stalls and amusements and side-shows there was only one that attracted her attention. It had curtains draped around, and outside sat a woman dressed all in black. There was a band around her forehead tying back her hair and, like Emma, she had about her the look of someone whose thoughts were far away.

"Good evening to you, Miss," she said when Emma drew near. "Wouldn't you like to come inside and uncover the secrets of your future?"

"It's a fortune-teller!" said Emma, looking appealingly at her grandfather. And somewhere in her thoughts a voice whispered: "I wonder if she could understand the mysteries of years gone by? I wonder if the tavern will appear in her crystal ball?"

Her grandfather took her arm and led her closer. "Let's see what handsome prince will win your heart and carry you off to his palace!"

The woman held open the curtain and beckoned her forward. "Come inside," she invited again. "There's little to pay for the secrets of tomorrow."

First the old man crossed her palm with silver. Then while he waited outside Emma and the fortune-teller sat facing each other at a table. One by one she turned over the tarot cards and set them before her, with gasps of surprise at what she found revealed there.

"You have a long life ahead of you," she foretold, "with much happiness – but some sadness, too."

Emma smiled nervously.

The woman's head was lowered, her eyes fixed on the cards. "Ah, what have we here? I see a journey to some place far, far away."

Emma looked at the woman in awe. "Far, far away? Will I travel across the sea?"

The fortune-teller seemed puzzled. "I see no oceans – no deserts," she said, peering more closely. "I see you only faintly, wandering . . . wandering. Going farther away in a mist . . ."

"Through the mists of time," Emma whispered, fearing that with another turn of the cards the woman would see her destination emerging from the shadows.

They both fell silent. Emma hesitated for a few moments, afraid to ask the question that was burning in her thoughts.

"When I wander far away," she said at last, "will I . . . will I be coming back again?"

CHAPTER 14

". . . Alone – and yet not alone . . ."

The fortune-teller laid the tarot cards on the table and invited Emma to select one. Then Emma watched while the lady in black turned them over one by one. All the while she spoke in mysterious tones.

"The cards show a dark man entering your life," the woman said. "One who brings much heartache." And this foretelling set Emma wondering whether it could be Evan Du who would again fill her heart with fear, or whether the figures depicted there revealed some other dark man – John, perhaps, grown tall and handsome, and from whom she would always be separated by the boundaries of time. It might be he who would bring her heartache.

"Is he dressed all in black, with a scar across his face?" she asked.

"Your fortune spells out only that he is dark."

Eagerly Emma's eyes searched the cards lying there. "Can you find two old women . . . or a boy calling for help . . . or a dreary old house with a lamp burning? . . ."

The fortune-teller frowned. "Two old women? . . . A scarred-faced man?" she echoed.

"A long time ago they lived in a shadowy house . . ." Emma began. She longed to tell of her adventures at Tŷ-yn-y-Cysgodion – of her journeys to that forgotten

place, and of a mystery which the woman might understand. But there was no time to recall each chapter. "It's
only a tale I've heard," she added meekly.

Her eyes lit up again when the fortune-teller uncovered
her crystal ball and peered into it. "I see a long road,
shrouded in mist and darkness," she said at length. "And
there's a light glowing in the distance."

"The lamplight in the attic window!" Emma imagined.
"Beckoning me there . . ."

But then, perhaps the misty road shows long months of
daydreams and loneliness, with a ray of happiness shining
in the future, thought Emma, a little disappointed.

"A light at the end of a journey," the woman muttered
on. "Not a journey over land and sea. A journey in your
dreams, perhaps – a longing to be far away. I see you
wandering along strange paths, not knowing which way to
go. You're looking all around . . . afraid . . . calling out
. . ."

Emma's heart was beating fast.

"There are shadows moving about you, like clouds
passing under the moon . . . figures with no clear shape."

She looked up, touching Emma's hand to reassure her.
"There's no danger," she promised. "The shadows are
sweeping through you – just as though you're not really
there at all."

"Am I lost? Shall I find my way back again?"

The fortune-teller peered closer. "Ah! Now the clouds
are drifting away, and the path is clear. I see hills and trees.
The light is behind you, growing faint. Your journey is
over, and you're wending your way home . . ."

"Am I alone?" Emma breathed, not wishing to break the
spell.

"Alone – and yet not alone. There's something moving

behind you – trying to catch up." She peered closer still. "It's all wrapped in mist – just like a ghost!"

Emma leaned across the table to peep into the crystal ball. As she did so, the fortune-teller replaced its covering of cloth.

"Once the images fade away, they never return," she said.

But in Emma's imagination the images were vivid – alive. Something moving behind – a ghostly shape following her, she reflected. Could it be that the fortune-teller shared her secret? That somehow she could reach beyond the bounds of time? In her confusion she wondered whether it was the Devil Sisters or Evan Du whom the woman had seen pursuing her. And Emma shuddered at the thought of it. Then she remembered John, imprisoned in the cellar. Perhaps some day she would discover a hidden path from Tŷ-yn-y-Cysgodion along which she could lead him to freedom. Maybe it was he who appeared in the crystal ball moving behind her.

"Don't be afraid," said the fortune-teller, as Emma rose from the table. "However far you travel you will never be alone. The people you meet on your journeys will always be near you."

And with the fortune-teller's parting words echoing in her thoughts, Emma went outside where her grandfather was waiting among the murmuring crowds.

Together they wandered on, around the market square and the field beyond, where lively side-shows attracted young folk and old. As the evening wore on, lanterns were lit to sway in the summer breeze; and groups of children ran here and there, revelling in the excitement of it all. But Emma was content to listen to their laughter and to watch them play, not wishing to join in the fun. After all, she had more than lantern lights and strains of music and sounds of gaiety to occupy her thoughts.

"What do your lucky stars foretell?" her grandfather smiled as they strolled along. "Are you to meet a handsome prince one day on your journey to some distant land?"

"Not a prince," Emma said absently. "A gipsy boy, perhaps. And who knows – maybe some day we will return together."

She told him all the fortune-teller had said.

Her grandfather put his arm around her shoulder, holding her attention for a while. "We all have our fantasies, my love," he began. "Hopes, and dreams of things we long for: dreams of riches when we're poor, of love when there's no one to care for us, a longing for adventure when we're lonely and life seems dreary. But the characters we sometimes build in our daydreams are only make-believe. They can never steal out of our imagination to become part of our everyday world."

"What if they were real characters, living in a different time?" said Emma. "Then they could appear as ghosts sometimes do."

The old man smiled. "What a crazy world it would be if those we dream of and ghosts from some other time were to become real folk and wander among us."

"Wouldn't that be wonderful!" Emma murmured wistfully; for if that were so John might be with her now, instead of trembling with fear in the cellar under the tavern, wondering if ever again he would see the light of day. Together they would be whirling on the merry-go-round or soaring on the swings above the crowds and rooftops, where the evening stars grew bright. They could run and laugh, happy as other children, without a care in the world.

125

"Not always so wonderful," her grandfather warned. "Sometimes frightful too! It's not only those from our dreams who would keep us company. The demons and devils of our nightmares would haunt us as well!"

Emma shuddered at the visions conjured by such a prospect – visions of Evan Du seeking her out, finding her in a dark corner, drawing so close that she could see only his eyes burning into hers.

"So, my love, the fortune-teller sees you setting out on a long journey," the old man went on, his voice becoming more cheerful as he changed the path of their conversation. "Somewhere far, far away? A strange journey, I should say, if you are to travel such a distance without crossing the oceans or the deserts."

"It's likely she means that I shall go far away only in my imagination," Emma interpreted. "Perhaps not many miles but many years away."

"Wherever you go, you must promise never to stay. Our hearts would be broken if we should lose you."

"I will always come back to you," Emma promised. Then, after a few moments' pondering, "'Alone – and yet not alone,' that's what the fortune-teller told me. She saw in her crystal ball something moving behind me. 'Something or someone all wrapped in mist, just like a ghost, following you on your homeward journey,' that's what she said. I wonder who that could be? Perhaps it's someone escaping from a place of make-believe or a time of long ago, and appearing here in the present – in the real world we understand."

The old man closed his eyes and slowly shook his head from side to side, not knowing how to answer her.

"It might be so," Emma persisted. "Often we wish we were somewhere else, and go there in our dreams. Maybe the people of somewhere else long to be here."

"Fortune-tellers are artful," her grandfather explained. "They learn more from looking into our eyes than gazing into their crystal ball. They understand our hopes and fears, and foretell only what we want to hear. Then one day we will return to them, and cross their palm with silver, to discover all the future happiness and adventure that lies in store for us."

"What if they see unhappiness or danger lying ahead?" Emma asked. "How would they read your fortune then?"

"Why, then they would wear an expression of mystery and tell how tomorrow was hidden in shadows and not easily uncovered. They prey on the superstition of the simple. You shouldn't believe all they say."

Emma was remembering the woman's prophecy. "Shadows moving about you, like clouds passing under the moon . . ." she had said. "A figure all wrapped in mist . . ." Could it mean that *her* tomorrows were so awesome that the fortune-teller was afraid to say more?

They strolled on among the crowd, not sharing its laughter and gaiety.

"Better be making our way home," the old man said. "It's past our supper time."

But Emma insisted that first they should search the stalls for some little keep-sake to take home for her grandmother. There was a variety of gifts to choose from, all displayed on the counters and shelves. Trinkets glistened in the lantern light; but most were cheap, gaudy – none that her grandmother might treasure.

From one stall to another Emma led the way while her grandfather followed patiently. And her search would have continued had not the sound of a voice that was vaguely familiar been heard among the crowd. Her heart leapt and she felt the colour drain from her cheeks as she looked around. For, standing there among a group of curious bystanders, she saw an elderly-looking gentleman wearing a three-quarter length coat and a wide-brimmed hat.

"Christian brothers and sisters," he was calling. "Spare a little of your time to listen to the word of God . . ."

Emma couldn't believe her eyes. "It can't be!" she whispered to herself. Then, venturing closer, she noticed the preacher's kindly smile and flowing, silver hair. She gaped in wonder. "But . . . it is! It's Old Josiah!"

CHAPTER 15

". . . She's come back again . . ."

Emma pushed her way through the circle of bystanders until she was so close to the preacher that she could have stretched out her hand and touched him. Bewildered, she stared into his face. There was no mistaking those grey eyes, the lilt of his voice. If it were not for the sound of music and laughter in the background, she could have pictured him standing beside the hearth in a far-off tavern, calling to those around him, begging alms for his church – just as he had done on the evening of his arrival at Tŷ-yn-y-Cysgodion. There were moments when she was inclined to tug at his coat to attract his attention. "Perhaps you have never seen me before," she would say, "but I remember your chestnut mare, Poll; and the boy who groomed her in the stable of a tavern once upon a time; and the Devil Sisters who stole into your room, watching you with eyes that glowed in the dark; and Evan Du pursuing you along the mountain paths . . ."

Then Old Josiah would perhaps look at her hard and long, as though some fearful memory had been awakened. "That was all a long time ago," she would remind him. "But it seemed to have happened only this summer."

But the preacher hardly glanced at her at all, and despite her tumbling thoughts Emma remained silent. After all,

she reflected, if somehow Old Josiah had escaped his
assailant on their journey to the county of Caernarfon, and
had lived on and on, then now he would be a very old man,
with wizened skin and back bent low. If he were dead and
gone and had come to haunt the country roads and streets
of town, then why was he not a misty shape with the
lantern lights of the fairground stalls shining through?
However, since he was neither a ghost nor an old, old man,
then what else but the wayward movement of time, leaping
crazily from one century to another, could account for his
appearance there?

"I come among you to spread His gospel," the preacher's
voice rambled on. "The goodness of the Lord knows no
bounds . . ." And Emma wondered whether the life span
of His disciple was boundless too.

Just then her grandfather came closer, and she felt his
hand upon her shoulder. "It's getting late," she heard him
say. So, with a last glance at the preacher whom she would
swear was the traveller she had known, Emma threaded
her way through the crowd. And her grandfather, noticing
how she was pale and trembling, put his arm around her.

In the corner of the market square they stopped for a
while at the stall of a flower seller, where Emma chose a
bunch of roses with their petals still unfurled. "Red roses
are for love," she remembered, and took them home for
her grandmother.

"Some day I shall be going on a long journey." Emma was
echoing the fortune-teller's prophecy as they sat down to
their supper. "And there I shall meet a dark man who will
bring me much heartache, so the picture cards foretell."

Mrs Dalamore lifted a steaming kettle from the fire. "A
journey?" she said absently. "Well now, that will be

exciting. Will you be going alone?"

"Yes, all alone, along some misty paths."

"Then it's the stranger you meet whose heart will be broken, I should imagine," her grandmother replied, mindful of her golden curls, her deep blue eyes and beguiling charm.

"A strange journey," Emma tried to explain. "Not a voyage across the sea. A dream journey perhaps. Why, you might hardly miss me at all!"

Her grandmother filled the teacups and passed them across the table. "A strange journey, indeed," she smiled. "You've been there many times before in your daydreams, I seem to recall; through howling winds and lightning storms and shadowy paths that lead to long ago and far away."

Emma looked from one to the other, lost in thought for a few moments. "But the fortune-teller could never have known," she said. "Not by looking into my eyes nor searching in her crystal ball. Perhaps my next journey will be different – more real than ever before."

"More real?"

"For a long time the woman gazed into her crystal ball, waiting for the images to become clearer. After a while she could make out a glowing light – the light that had guided me on my way to wherever I was travelling." She lowered her voice, as though her grandparents should also wonder at the mystery of the fortune-teller's revelations. "Now the light was behind me, growing faint in the distance . . ."

"Well, I never!" her grandmother interrupted, with an affected gasp of astonishment. "She could see you returning from your journey – waking from your dream, I shouldn't wonder."

Emma was not to be discouraged. "But this time I was

not alone," she continued. "The fortune-teller shielded her eyes to look closer. 'I can see shadows moving about you,' she said. 'Figures with no clear shape . . . all wrapped in mist – just like ghosts!'"

Occasionally her grandparents glanced at each other across the table, raising their eyebrows, smiling tolerantly as Emma rambled on.

"There was no need to fear, she told me. However far I travelled I should never be alone, because the people I met on my journey would always be near." She frowned thoughtfully. "I wonder what she meant by that?"

"Perhaps she means that you will attract new friends wherever you go," her grandfather suggested.

Emma pondered. The woman's foretelling was deeper than that, she felt sure. "Could it be," she ventured, "that it really was a ghost appearing in her crystal ball? Someone who lived long ago coming back to haunt me?" She could think of no other explanation for Old Josiah's presence at the fair.

"It simply means that always you will be very precious to those who love you," her grandfather teased, ruffling her hair as he usually did whenever she drifted off into her daydreams. Then, to change the trend of the conversation, he examined the roses arranged in a vase and now standing on the table before them. "She chose them herself," he said, admiring their fragrance and deep colour. "'Red roses for someone I love,' she said, and bought them especially for you, Nell."

Emma was reflecting still on the mysterious appearance of Old Josiah – or else someone who bore a startling resemblance to him. She wished she could tell of the preacher whom she had known, but then they would breathe deep sighs and chide her all the more. So she took the secret to bed with her, and lay there wondering and wondering, her thought at last drifting into dreams.

Emma had always known that the House in the Shadows might beckon her at any hour of the day or night. In some unguarded moment it would call her away. It was never she who chose the time to come or go. While she slept that night, its black fingers stretched out to snatch her back.

When Emma awoke and opened her eyes there was still darkness all round her. Where she lay was hard and cold to her touch. Once in a while she was startled by a faint screeching and the scampering of rats nearby. She shuddered, scrambling to her feet, groping around in the unfamiliar surroundings.

"Emma? Emma – is that you?" It was John's voice calling to her through the darkness: the darkness of the cellar where Evan Du had imprisoned him. It seemed now such a long time ago, Emma thought; but likely just a little while to John. She felt her way along the wall, following the sound of his voice. "My hands are bound fast. Emma – where are you?"

"I'll untie them," Emma called back; and then suddenly she realised that there in her Otherworld she was just a shadow – a ghostly person whom only the boy could hear or see. There was little she could do to help.

"He's gone now; but soon he'll be back again," said John, as though it had been only a moment ago that Evan Du's footsteps grew fainter as he climbed the steps. She thought it strange too that John did not ask why she had deserted him – where she had been these past weeks. There was, of course, only one explanation. This was yet another mystery in the passing of time she would never understand.

Gradually Emma's eyes became accustomed to the

darkness, and in the thin shaft of light that filtered under the door she could make out John's silhouette. He was sitting in the corner, leaning forward, with his hands raised to his face, trying to untie the kerchief which bound him by tugging at the knots with his teeth. Her efforts to help were futile, for her fingers passed through his wrists as freely as shadows moving over the ground. She remembered when she had first come upon the boy in his attic room: how he had described her misty shape beyond which the candle-light showed, almost as clearly as though she were not there at all. How often had others passed directly through her whenever she stood in their path!

"Perhaps I could just as easily pass through the door or the walls that surround me!" Emma considered excitedly, surprised that the idea had not occurred to her before.

She approached the cellar door through the darkness, stepped forward with some uncertainty, and the next instant found herself at the foot of the steps which led up to the tavern. The door at the top was wide open, allowing the daylight to come streaming down.

There was not a sound from the tavern as Emma ascended the steps. She wandered along the passages, up the stairs, and through doors she had never dared enter before. The rooms sometimes used to shelter overnight travellers were all darkened by shutters fastened against the windows. Each was barely furnished, and dusty cobwebs hung grey from the ceiling and spanned the alcoves. From one to another she roamed, with never a murmur to break the silence, passing through the doors and walls, from sunlight to shade, as ghosts are said to do.

When she came upon the room where Old Josiah had spent a night of terror she found it still in disarray. A chair and candlestick were overturned. The fireplace was blackened with soot which had fallen from the chimney. And the bedclothes, torn and daubed with blood, lay strewn about the floor. Had she known of the fearful struggle that occurred during the night she would have stared into the corners of the room and above the wardrobe, expecting to see two pairs of eyes burning there.

For a long time she wandered around, always watching and listening. But of Evan Du, who had left John bound in the cellar, there was no sign.

Her silent exploration continued. She stole past the door of the Devil Sisters' room, moving to the other side of the corridor; for although she was an intruder, she remembered occasions when Jessie, with her second sight and witching wiles, seemed also to be aware of her presence.

Presently she made her way back down the stairs, still puzzling for some way by which she could help John escape; wondering where his captor might be, so that she could give some warning of his return. When the tavern was open he was usually to be found drinking ale in raucous company. And many a night, so it seemed, he had neither the strength nor the inclination to rise from his chair in the *simne fawr;* sleeping there instead until the fire burned low.

The place Evan Du called his own was an old woodman's shack just beyond the stables. Here he stowed his scant possessions, hidden away in a seafarer's bag.

But now the tavern was deserted, except perhaps for Agatha and Jessie, secluded in their room. And Emma was as loath to venture near their door as to seek out the shack where Evan Du might be waiting.

At length she passed through the door at the back of the tavern and wandered across the cobbled yard towards a clearing in the trees. From here she had a view of the valley

135

for miles along. Scanning the green slopes she saw at first only flecks of white here and there, and heard the distant bleating of the sheep on the hillside. Then, farther away, high on the shoulder of the hill, there appeared a silhouette that brought a gasp of joy to her lips. "She's come back again!" she cried, raising a hand to her forehead to hide the glare of the sun. "Poll has come looking for her master!"

CHAPTER 16

" . . . Come inside, my pretty . . ."

In her excitement, Emma ran forward waving her arms wildly and calling out at the top of her voice: "Poll! Come on, girl!" It was almost as though the mare heard her call, for she tore at the ground with her hooves, whinnied, and then came forward at a trot. Down into the valley she came, closer and closer, until Emma could make out her chestnut coat against the green of the hills, and see the reins dangling at her neck. "Come on, girl!" she called again.

Before long the mare appeared among the trees, more hesitant now, pausing to look about, snorting, fidgeting restively. Emma's voice softened. "Good old Poll. Don't be frightened. There's no one to harm you."

Warily, the mare approached the stables, her ears erect, listening for some sound beyond the open door. Then she ventured through the doorway, with never a glance in the girl's direction. Even when Emma went close to stroke her, she started only momentarily and then lowered her head to drink from the water trough.

It was while Emma was looking out from the doorway of the stable that she first saw the shack among the trees, and someone inside moving past the window. Soon afterwards the door opened and Evan Du emerged, with his seafarer's bag slung over his shoulder. His cruel expression sent a shiver down Emma's spine; and when she noticed the spade he was carrying a cry of horror escaped her lips. She had visions of John being buried in the cellar in the same way as other unfortunate victims, so that they could never bear witness to his crimes.

Across the yard and into the tavern she ran, crying out her warning, not caring whether she was seen or heard. She fled along the passage and down the steps, passing through the door and back into the darkness of the cellar.

"Evan Du . . . He's coming!" she gasped, for his footsteps were not far behind her. A few moments later the door burst open and he was standing there framed in the daylight. Emma backed into the corner beside John.

He came towards the boy, taking his knife from its sheath and holding its point so close against John's throat that it drew a trickle of blood. "Don't make a sound!" he warned. And Emma and John were frozen with terror.

They watched him bolt the door, move into the depths of the cellar, and there light a lamp which he took to an alcove in the farthest wall. Then he dislodged some of the stones that paved the cellar floor and began digging into the earth beneath them.

"He's making a grave!" Emma cried in desperation, urging John to run for his life, forgetting that with the door bolted he was trapped inside. She groped feverishly at the kerchief that bound him, and then rushed to the door, fumbling at the bolt. But all her efforts were in vain.

At length, Evan Du threw aside the spade and kneeled over the pit he had dug. After rummaging in the earth, he dragged from its hiding place a wooden chest. Then he brought the lamp closer, raised the lid and ran his fingers through the contents, all the while chuckling to himself.

"What's he found?" Emma whispered, fearing that the bones of some past victim had been unearthed.

"It's all the possessions he's stolen and hidden away," said John. "A buried treasure, I shouldn't wonder."

Then, as Evan Du delved deeper into the chest, scooping out handfuls of plunder to fill his seafarer's bag, they saw golden coins and an assortment of jewellery glistening in the lamplight.

For a long while he kneeled there, gloating over his ill-gotten hoard, stuffing into his bag as much as he could carry, loath to leave any of his treasure behind.

"He'll never get away from them," said John. "No one can escape the spells of Agatha and Jessie. They can watch over the woods with the eyes of hawks. Wherever he goes they will follow."

Emma's eyes were fixed on the thief as he lowered the chest into the ground and replaced the paving stones. She feared that before his task was done and he set off over the hills, another grave would be dug in the cellar floor, and his only witness would be buried there.

"What if . . . if there's no one to tell?" For a moment Emma thought that somehow Evan Du had overheard her, because it was then that he returned to the corner where the boy lay.

Standing over John, he grasped the handle of the knife hanging at his belt. "Remember what I say, gipsy boy," he warned. "I'm leaving this miserable place forever. Going off across the sea where I belong, and taking with me only what's mine . . ." He raised his eyes to the ceiling and pointed toward the tavern. "One word of what you've seen – one whisper to the old crones and . . ." He drew his knife from its sheath and brandished it menacingly.

"I shall . . . shall never tell!" John stammered. "If . . . if only you will untie my hands and set me free, *I* shall never tell where you've gone."

"And there'd be no thief and murderer for the Devil Sisters to send in pursuit!" said Emma bitterly, for believing now that no one save John could hear her voice made her bold.

Evan Du came closer, clutching at the boy's clothes and staring into his face. "You'll be here for always!" he snarled. "They'll never let you go – not while there's wood to cut for fires, and stables to clean . . ." He shook him fiercely. "If I had my way! . . ."

"I'll never tell! I promise – never!" John cried.

"If I'd had my way you'd be buried down here in the cellar with the rats to gnaw at your bones!" He lowered his voice, turning to look towards the door. "There's not a living soul I fear – none that roams the hills or sails the seas . . ." Once again he paused to listen and look over his shoulder. "None but two old women who sit in their dark room, muttering and brooding all day long. I'm thinking they're not of flesh and blood like ordinary folk!"

"The Devil Sisters, I've heard them called," said John, glancing at Emma.

"Aye, she-devils right enough. Cunning as two vixens. Always hatching some mischief or other. Nothing escapes their sharp eyes. It's those spells they keep whispering – witchery, and that cursed looking-glass hanging in the corner of their room!"

"Looking-glass?" murmured Emma, her eyes bright with interest.

"No secrets are hidden from them," John remembered ruefully.

Evan Du scowled. "Unless you do as I bid," he threatened, "never again will you see the light of day.

There's no one to fret over you. You'll just lie forgotten in an unmarked grave!"

Like other poor souls, Emma reflected, whom they had robbed and murdered in the past.

John shrank farther into the corner, trembling with fright. "Whatever you say," he promised, "if only you will set me free. I'll go far away and take your secret with me."

Evan Du stooped beside the boy and untied his hands. Then his lips curled in a sinister smile, for he knew full well that John was not to escape so easily; that the errand upon which he was to embark was fraught with danger. "You'll have to be as cunning as the she-devils themselves," he said, as he spelled out the task to be accomplished.

Up the stairs and along the corridor John was to steal, and there enter the room of the Devil Sisters. Hanging at the wall in the corner he would see a looking-glass, with a warped face and filmed with dust. Like the fortune-teller's crystal ball, whenever Agatha and Jessie chose to peer into its depths and invoke its mystic powers, it would reveal secrets hidden from others.

"Creep through the door, quiet as a shadow!" John was warned; for if he were caught meddling in their spells, likely he would in an instant wither away like the autumn leaves. "Unfasten the looking-glass from its hook in the wall, and fetch it to me. They will have no second sight when it's smashed to a thousand pieces!" Then the Devil Sisters would be blind to all that happened beyond the confines of their room, he explained with a mischievous grin; and, with their spells broken, he could escape, unhindered. "I'll be rid of this place forever!" he cried. "And rich for the rest of my days!"

It was then that John fully realised the difficulty of his task and the danger it involved. He dare not enter the room of Agatha and Jessie.

"They hear every sound!" he trembled. "However quietly I open the door they are sure to find me there. They never leave their room until after dark. And whenever they do they lock the door behind them and take away the key!"

"Would you rather rot forever in the cellar!" threatened Evan Du. "If they find you there, then snatch the looking-glass from the wall and run like the wind!"

A sudden notion filled Emma's thoughts. "If the spells of the Devil Sisters are broken . . ." she whispered. "If they can no longer watch out over the hills and woods – then maybe we can escape ourselves!" But then other thoughts crept into her mind, and she fell to wondering of old tales of mystery where witches were known to conjure pictures in the flames that lick the fire-grate. It seemed that John was between the Devil and the deep blue sea.

It was not long before the grin vanished from Evan Du's face and he began to look more fierce than ever. He slung his bag of treasure over his shoulder and slid back the bolt; but before opening the door he seized John's arm and held him fast. "Remember your promise, gipsy boy. Steal upstairs, quiet as a shadow. Listen at their door and watch for your chance. If they should huddle in the hearth over some witch's brew and turn their backs upon you – then is the time to creep into the corner. Take the cursed looking-glass and bring it back to me in my shack." His grip on John's arm tightened. "Should you come back without it, or breathe a word of what you've seen, you'll smother in your grave before nightfall. Run away and I'll find you wherever you hide. Even if I fall under the she-devils' spell and turn to stone or crumble to dust, the ghost of Evan Du will never let you rest! I'll haunt you all your days! No matter where you are, I'll find you – and all your dreams will be nightmares!"

He stared at the boy as he uttered his threats; and Emma, standing nearby, felt his eyes burning through her, as though she were to share his grave warning. She shuddered at the thought of it, until the door was opened and a shaft of daylight came pouring down upon them.

It was with a curious feeling both of relief and apprehension that Emma and John mounted the cellar steps – thankful to escape the darkness of their prison, and with a dread of what they might encounter in that room along the corridor upstairs.

"Poll has found her way back to the stable," Emma remembered. "We could gallop off together."

But the footsteps of Evan Du were not far behind, and his eyes were watching.

"He'll find the mare and ride away on her himself," John realised despondently. "He'll not care what happens to me so long as he and his treasure are safe from their clutches. Once their spell is broken he will have no mercy."

John was not out of his captor's sight until Evan Du passed through the door at the back of the tavern, leaving the boy, with Emma beside him, to climb the stairs alone.

Together they moved along the corridor with much misgiving. Indeed, it was only the fearful threats still tumbling through their thoughts that held them to their task, for there were moments when they were tempted to steal back down the stairs, hurry through the front door, and then run on and on until they reached the shelter of the woods. But they knew in their hearts that the shady paths could never lead them beyond the spells of the Devil Sisters nor the vengeance of Evan Du.

Listening in the corridor, they heard no sound from

143

within the room. The door was ajar, creaking softly as John pushed it open a little wider. He peered through the narrow gap, too frightened to pass beyond the threshold. Emma, too, could feel her heart beating fast as she took a step forward, and then another, for she had discovered now that no walls or doors could bar her way.

The room was dimly lit, as though nightfall were approaching. The curtains drawn across the window shut out the brightness of day, allowing only chinks of sunlight to filter through. One of the sisters was hunched in a chair beside the fire, so still that Emma imagined she was asleep. For a while the other was nowhere to be seen. It was a voice coming from a corner of the room that attracted Emma's attention to a dark shape moving there.

"Come inside, my pretty," someone was saying.

CHAPTER 17

". . . They've set their mark on him . . ."

"I know you're here somewhere, my fair one," the voice continued. "Where are you hiding?" Jessie stretched out her arms, groping about the room as though she sensed a presence she could not see. "Wake up, Agatha. I'm thinking we have a visitor."

Emma stood quite still, not daring to move for fear of betraying her whereabouts. Yet even when Jessie came close enough to touch her there was not a spark of recognition in her eyes. Emma was aware only of a strange sensation when Jessie's hands and body passed right through her.

Agatha wakened; and together the sisters searched the room for the ghostly intruder, once in a while returning to the corner where Jessie had been peering into the looking-glass that hung on the wall. "A young maid," she went on. "So faint and misty. Maybe a ghost has come a calling." And then aloud, turning to look about her: "Where are you, my pretty? What do you want with two old souls in a lonely house?"

"I want to travel years away – to the place where I belong," Emma longed to say. "If you can weave magic spells, then let the gipsy boy go free. Help him to escape so that he can come with me." But she was too afraid to answer them at all. Instead she clung to the shadows, watching, listening.

Presently the old women made their way to the door and looked along the corridor. But already John had stolen away, seeking refuge in his room in the attic, for he feared the Devil Sisters and their sorcery even more than Evan Du.

In the corner where Jessie and Agatha had huddled together, Emma could see the looking-glass – the talisman that mirrored pictures hidden from all save the sisters' eyes. To her it seemed an ordinary glass before which they might stand to brush their hair. Now it reflected only the glow of the fire and empty chairs beside the hearth.

While the old women were peering along the corridor, Emma moved closer, passing in front of the glass; but her image did not appear there. Even when she raised her hand to touch it, nothing flickered in the reflection of the room except a flame licking the bars of the fire-grate and a curtain stirring in the breeze. It had not the magic of a fortune-teller's crystal ball, she decided, somewhat disenchanted. Before long, however, the looking-glass was to unveil pictures that roused the Devil Sisters to anger and made Emma gasp with wonder.

"Well, upon my soul!" Agatha sighed as she shuffled back inside the room, tapping her stick along the floor. "I'm thinking some poor waif can find no rest and has wandered here to haunt us."

They drew open the curtains and let the daylight stream in. But although they had found Emma's likeness in their looking-glass, elsewhere there was no sign of the girl they were seeking.

"Where are you, my pretty?" Jessie called out again. "What brings you to an old tavern in the woods?"

Emma did not answer them. She stood still and silent in the corner, as ghosts are often said to do.

When their searching was over they closed the curtains, and once again the room was darkened. It was then that the sisters began to weave their spell. Murmuring incantations to invoke the spirits of what they called the *Dirgelaidd Dwr* (Mysterious Waters) and *Pwll Cyfareddol* (Magic Pool), they sprinkled upon the fire some concoction which coloured the flames and sent clouds of purple smoke billowing up the chimney. There was a crackling and spluttering, and sweet-smelling fumes filled the room.

". . . *Dirgelaidd Dwr* . . . *Pwll Cyfareddol* . . ." Emma could hear them muttering in their spell, and wondered what spirits they were calling upon, for she knew of no myterious waters or magic pool near the tavern.

Across the room the two old witches moved, to the corner where Emma hid. And the nearer they came the faster her heart was beating. But they passed her by without a glance, and approached the looking-glass. At first Emma saw only their reflections staring back at her; and it seemed for a moment as though their images were two other witches who had come to keep them company or gather like a coven.

Her imagination was running wild. She wondered why the images were still, while the Devil Sisters turned their heads to look around; why the reflections of the fire and the furniture in the room had vanished. Could it be that she was looking through a window into somewhere conjured by the sisters' spell?

Then, as Emma watched, a strange thing happened, and she was more bewildered than ever. The reflections of Agatha and Jessie became distorted as the surface of the looking-glass rippled and swirled like a pool into which a

147

stone had been thrown.

"... *Diregelaidd Dwr* ... *Pwll Cyfareddol* ..." she heard recited again in the Devil Sisters' mutterings; and gradually the shimmering in the glass ceased, and the ruffling on its surface calmed. Then, from that Somewhere beyond, different scenes emerged, one following another like someone flicking through the pictures in a story book. One moment there appeared a reflection of the stairway leading from the tavern; then the corridor above, with a shaft of light slanting through the window at the far end. Not a soul was visible in the looking-glass, even though Agatha and Jessie were standing directly in front of it: no one, until the scene changed to the attic room where John could be seen listening at the door. He seemed frightened hiding there, not knowing where else to seek refuge.

"Maybe this wraith is roaming abroad and spreads fear through the house," Agatha chuckled.

Before long, however, both she and Jessie were to peer intently, and purse their lips in anger at the revelation in their *Pwll Cyfareddol*. Its surface rippled once more, and when it cleared an image of Evan Du appeared there. He was waiting in his shack among the trees. His eyes shone with greed as he ran his fingers through the golden coins and pieces of jewellery stuffed in his seafarer's bag.

"*Gwas y Diafol!*" (Servant of the Devil) They muttered curses under their breath; their fingers curled like talons. "He's dug up our treasure chest to keep for himself!"

"Thief!" Agatha croaked.

"He'll rue the day!" hissed Jessie, already plotting vengeance.

Together they returned to the hearth, there to kindle the fire with shrivelled berries, herbs and mouldy toadflax, until it crackled and flared, and blue flames licked the

grate. It was while they wove some evil spell that Emma
stole away and hurried to John in the attic.

"The looking-glass is bewitched!" she called to him as
she was climbing the stairs. "It ripples just as the water in a
pool; and curious pictures are reflected there!" She was
beside him now, her eyes wide with astonishment.
"Pictures changing all the time like a magic lantern or a
crystal ball! Whatever they wished to see appeared there
. . ." She moved her hands helplessly, as though she could
not explain further. "If only I could have snatched it from
the wall . . ."

"Nothing is hidden from the Devil Sisters' eyes," John
said despondently. "They can even look into tomorrow and
tell what the future holds."

Almost an hour passed before they plucked up the
courage to creep down the stairs. From the old women's
room they heard a murmured chant, and trembled to think
what fearful web they spun to snare their victim.

The clock on the tavern wall showed that the day was
slipping away. Before long, farmers would be leaving their
fields and wending their way over the hills to quench their
thirst at Tŷ-yn-y-Cysgodion. If Evan Du were to make off,
unnoticed, with his stolen treasure he dare not wait till
sunset. John could well imagine his fury when he learned
that the looking-glass still hung in the Devil Sisters' room
and their spell had not been broken. He knew too that he
would pay for his failure with his life. Evan Du's threats
were burning in his thoughts, and he was so afraid that he
startled at every creak and moving shadow. "Come back
without it, and before nightfall you'll smother in your
grave!" he had been warned. "Run away, and I'll find you
wherever you hide . . . Evan Du will never let you rest. I'll
haunt you always . . . always!"

"What shall I do?" the boy asked Emma in despair. And it worried her to read the fear in his eyes.

"He'll not trouble us any longer," Emma said to console him. "Agatha and Jessie have set their mark on him. Even now he has fallen under their spell, I shouldn't wonder. When night-time comes he'll vanish into the darkness, never to be seen again!"

John laughed nervously, imagining some awesome curse transforming the villain into a black rat, to screech in torment, scurrying about the cellar for all time, among the casks of ale and the shallow graves of ill-fated travellers.

"Perhaps his ghost will be doomed to haunt the House in the Shadows," said Emma. Then, seeing the fear rekindled in John's eyes, she added quickly: "But when he's gone, there'll be no one to follow when we run away!"

John sighed, remembering that Evan Du had not yet been spirited away. Somewhere he was awaiting the boy's return – at any moment likely to appear before him.

From the back door they peeped across the yard, first toward the shack, where nothing stirred. Then they looked toward the open door of the stable.

"Listen!" Emma whispered, when she heard a sound coming from inside. "It's Poll – still waiting there!"

Sensing that someone was near, the mare became uneasy, shuffling her hooves on the stable floor. John edged forward, clicking his tongue and calling to her softly. "Come on Poll. Easy, girl; there's no one to harm you." He approached cautiously, not wanting to startle her, for he knew that Old Josiah's mare was his last chance of escape.

She did not shy away when John came close and stretched out his hand to stroke her mane. Instead, she tossed her head from side to side and then lowered it again to munch at a bundle of hay. Emma, too, patted her neck and wondered whether the mare could feel her fingers upon her chestnut coat. "Shall she be ours, to keep for always?" she said wistfully. And then, while John arranged the saddle and bridle in readiness for their journey, Emma kept watch at the stable door, many times looking over her shoulder, urging the boy to hurry.

It was she who cried out in alarm when she caught sight of Evan Du emerging from his shack. Desperately, John ran from the stable, leading Poll by the reins. But no sooner had he climbed into the saddle than Evan Du was upon him, seizing the halter and throwing the rider to the ground. John scrambled to his feet and fled toward the woods, with his assailant calling after him: "I'll find you, gipsy boy! I'll not forget your mischief. There's nowhere you can hide from Evan Du!"

"Run, John – run!" Emma screamed, as she watched him disappear among the trees.

Evan Du did not at once set off in pursuit. He laid his seafarer's bag across the mare's back and fastened it to the saddle. Then, with a furtive glance toward the upstairs windows of the tavern, he mounted the mare, viciously digging his heels into her flanks.

At first the poor beast was frightened. But then, as her tormentor tugged at the reins and lashed them across her face, it seemed that Poll was suddenly possessed by some devil. With nostrils flared and eyes blazing, she reared and flailed the air with her fore-hooves, toppling Evan Du from the saddle. All the while she let out a frenzied cry, trampling upon the fallen rider as he struggled to rise. Time and again her hooves descended with an amazing fury, until there lay on the cobblestones a crumpled form that Emma could barely recognise. Even still, the beast raged and

151

whinnied incessantly. But Evan Du would never stir again.

In all the commotion, Emma was aware of voices nearby crying out in alarm. The incident outside the stable had startled some neighbouring farmers who were already approaching the tavern to quench their thirst. Now they were gathered around, staring in horror, waving their arms to drive off the furious mare. It was then that Emma raised her eyes to the upstairs window where two old women were huddled together, looking down and chuckling to themselves.

The swell of the farmers' voices, the shrill whinnying of Poll and the sound of her own sobbing echoed in her ears and then grew fainter, moment by moment, as though somehow Tŷ-yn-y-Cysgodion and all the happenings there were drifting farther and farther away.

The black fingers which had stretched out to snatch her from her sleep now carried her home and laid her in her bed again.

CHAPTER 18

. . . not a soul at the funeral . . .

It was not long before Emma was to return to her Otherworld, and as had happened sometimes in the past, her journey began in the quiet and darkness of the night when she was alone in her room, dreaming of the shadowy house and those who dwelt within its walls. On this occasion, however, time at Tŷ-yn-y-Cysgodion had not stood still to wait for her. It had moved to some distant past. It was summer, as usually it seemed to be whenever she found herself wandering there. But now it was a far-off summer, longer ago than ever before. She recognised the woods and hills, yet where Tŷ-yn-y-Cysgodion had stood there was only a dell – a clearing among the trees where reeds grew tall in the shade.

From somewhere in the dell came the sound of voices – children's voices, it seemed, singing or chanting together, although there was no one to be seen. As Emma drew closer they came into view: a group of girls no older than she, their hands joined one with another, skipping merrily around a pool and calling in song to the spirit of the *Dirgelaidd Dwr*. Several times they circled the water. Then, one by one, they fell to their knees and peered into its depths, with sighs or gasps of wonder; for at their beckoning a reflection of their true-love was to appear there, to vanish again when they bent low to touch the surface with their lips.

For some time their chanting and dancing continued, with laughter and cries of excitement. Curious, Emma moved forward to join in their fun. But, as had always happened before, not a glance was cast in her direction.

As she approached, the girls left their play and ran from the pool as though someone hidden at the edge of the woods had called to them. Emma began to follow, but stopped suddenly beside the water, holding her breath when she recognised two old women standing in their midst. Although the years had rolled back, longer ago than her journeys to the tavern, there was no mistaking their familiar appearance – ragged clothes trailing to the ground, one woman tall, the other bent and leaning on a stick. It was the Devil Sisters standing there: the ageless Agatha and Jessie, never a day younger despite the backward movement of time. And the bright-eyed girls were gathered about them like moths round a candle flame.

Emma watched them until her attention was drawn to a stirring of the water. For a few moments its surface ruffled and then was calm again, throwing out the strangest reflections. These were constantly changing, some lingering longer than others. She stared, bewildered, at what she saw in the *Dirgelaidd Dwr* – scenes of winter and summer, daytime and moonlight, all passing swiftly. Mirrored in the depths of the pool, time was bounding crazily from past to future. Once Emma glimpsed the tangle of a primeval forest; then bare hills with valleys beyond.

It was all so mysterious. Stranger still – and appearing there for a minute or more – was the image of a house, or rather of its charred remains. Familiar in its outline, and lying in the shadow of surrounding trees . . . "Why, surely," Emma whispered to herself, "that's the ruins of Tŷ-yn-y-Cysgodion!"

This last image was slow to fade; and when it had gone, the pool vanished with it. As Emma looked about her again, there was no one to be seen. Instead, she found herself on the path through the woods; and the tavern was there ahead of her, as large as life, fully clothed in its coat of ivy, and its door opened wide to welcome her.

On this occasion time had moved forward since she was last there. It was long past sunset. The lamps which hung from the beams across the ceiling were unlit, and only candle flames were flickering all about the room, with halos of light that shone on the faces of those gathered there. They sat in groups around the tables, drinking mugs of ale, talking noisily, sometimes breaking into song. Except for the candle-light, and the absence of a scarred-faced man dressed in black, it was a scene similar to that which Emma had encountered when first she came upon Tŷ-yn-y-Cysgodion.

No one thought it odd that a young girl should wander among them for, of course, she was invisible to all save John and – she remembered with a start – the Devil Sisters when they searched for reflections in their looking-glass. No one stood behind the counter where Evan Du was usually seen. When their mugs were empty the men in the tavern replenished their drinks themselves from the casks of ale which now flowed freely. Everyone was absorbed in the merry-making. Emma made her way to the far end of the room and began to climb the stairs. Then a voice called excitedly from the corridor above. "Emma! I was afraid I should never see you again!" John was looking down at her over the banister rail. "Every day I have been watching for you – wondering where you were."

Emma could not explain how she had vanished from the nightmare outside the stable, nor where she had been, nor why time had hurried on while she was away. "I remember Poll whinnying and kicking out wildly – and Evan Du lying there . . ." She shuddered, as though trying to shut out the memory of it all.

"He's gone," John sighed. "He'll never trouble us again." He looked beyond Emma, to the flickering flames in the tavern, which lit up the faces of the people gathered there.

"I don't understand," she said, peering down into the dimly lit room.

They were together now, watching from the top of the stairs; and once in a while John looked behind him towards the door of the Devil Sisters' room where, as always, a light was showing underneath.

"Why are the candles burning, and everyone singing?" asked Emma.

"*Gwylnos* – a Wake Night," said the boy. "It's the custom: always on the eve of a funeral."

"But who would mourn for Evan Du? He was so wicked and cruel; and no one will be sad at his passing away."

John shrugged his shoulders, not knowing how to explain. "It's the custom with country folk," he told her again. Then he tried to describe how, at a Gwylnos, it is usually the practice for friends and relatives of the deceased to gather together the night before the burial to celebrate the dead person's release from pain and mortal cares. This they did with song and drink and brief lamentations. And of Evan Du there would be memories only of his evil ways, John agreed. "Perhaps they come because tonight the ale is free," he added cynically, "and sing because they're glad he's gone forever!"

"There was no Gwylnos for Old Josiah," Emma reflected bitterly. "It's likely he was buried in some unmarked grave, and is already forgotten."

Then, for a while, she fell silent, remembering how the preacher who once lay murdered at the roadside had mysteriously appeared among the crowds at the fair. She recalled, too, the fortune-teller's warning that however far she wandered, the people she met on her journey would never be far away – even when her travels were over. "I see them as ghostly shapes, following through the mists of time," she had foretold. And now Emma began to fear that her prophesy might come true. Could it be, she wondered, that when they were dead and gone some lived on in another time? Would the ghost of a black-hearted seafarer some day come to haunt her?

"Old Josiah was just a lonely traveller," said John. "Only we saw him die, and no one will remember him. But Evan Du was known for miles around – and feared by most!"

Once more he glanced along the corridor, as if he were expecting a door to open and two old women emerge from their room. "It wasn't the poor beast that killed him," he went on. "Poll was bewitched by some demon they called upon! Likely they cast a spell or mixed some devil's brew and . . ."

"Is she hurt? Did Poll go free?" Emma interrupted.

In answer to her questions, John lowered his voice and retold the fearful happenings of that afternoon behind the tavern; for in all the confusion – the fury of the mare and the cries of the farmers as they strove to drive her off – he had paid little attention to Emma. He told of a beast possessed, rearing and foaming at the mouth, unceasingly trampling upon her tormentor until his struggles were over.

And when, at last, they held her at bay, Evan Du lay still in a pool of blood.

"I heard the crying and shouting," Emma remembered. "Then the sounds grew faint, as if I were waking from a dream."

"They carried him indoors and laid the body on a table," John continued. "Then Agatha and Jessie came shuffling down the stairs, wondering whatever had come over the furious beast, and wherever had it come from. But when no one was watching there was a sparkle in their eyes and a smile on their lips!"

"Did Poll run away?" Emma asked again.

Just then there was a creak as a door behind them opened and the light spilled out. Startled, John hid in the darkness of the stairs leading to his room in the attic and Emma moved beside him. There they watched and waited in silence while the Devil Sisters passed by, clutching the banister rail as they descended to the tavern, for it was customary at a Gwylnos for everyone within the house to gather in the candle-light.

"Even now they're chuckling at their mischief," Emma whispered, when the sisters had gone farther down the stairs.

The old women were out of sight before they came from their hiding-place and John told the end of his story; and as it unfolded, tears of compassion came to Emma's eyes.

"Afterwards the farmers beat Poll with sticks and shut her in the stable, frightened and all alone. Then, as night wore on, Agatha and Jessie went to her, to unfasten the seafarer's bag from the saddle and drive the mare off into the woods. I saw them take their treasure back to the cellar . . ."

Emma heard no more. Her thoughts were filled with

visions of Poll, still all alone and frightened, wandering the hills in search of her master. "We must find her!" she resolved. And even though there were only stars and a slim crescent of moonlight to show the way, she would have gone whistling and calling through the night, along the valley and over the shoulders of the hills, trusting that somehow her ghostly voice would echo far.

She was half-way down the stairs when an unusual sound prompted her to stop and listen. Some of the people in the tavern heard it too, for gradually their singing and noisy banter ceased, until all were silent, looking from one to another, listening to the sound growing louder.

It seemed that a stampede of frightened beasts was approaching – galloping helter-skelter, with shrill cries and thundering hooves. It was quite unlike the sound of earthly creatures. Eyes peered from the tavern windows searching the darkness; but nothing was seen stirring in the woods. For a while Emma imagined that the trees themselves had torn their roots from the ground and came pounding upon the house, their limbs flapping like the wings of monstrous birds, and owls staring from the boughs screeching out in terror.

Then the door burst open and the candles were blown out by an icy wind, uncommon on a summer night. For a while the tavern was filled with murmuring voices and darkness. This was followed by moments of silence. Then the thundering hooves and eerie sounds were heard again, noisily at first, outside the doorway. The furniture rattled, toppling mugs of ale to the floor; and Emma felt the banister rail tremble.

"I saw a beast with horns and eyes burning like fire!" cried someone at the window. "It's the Hounds of Hell baying in the woods!" swore another.

Whatever had come to the doors of Tŷ-yn-y-Cysgodion was now moving away, for the sounds of it were fading in the distance. Then all was quiet again. One by one the candles were relit, and Emma could see Jessie and Agatha huddled together near the fireplace. While others were looking about in fear, their shoulders were rocking with laughter, as though they well understood the purpose of such a frightful visitation.

"Drink up, and make merry!" came Agatha's husky voice, as she waved her stick about. "Don't be afearing – it's not you who's going to the grave!"

John's face was pale as death. "Perhaps it's the Devil coming to take him away!" he whispered.

Many left the tavern and hurried out into the night. Some stayed until the first cock crowed, drinking and singing farewell to Evan Du before his last voyage.

The next morning a hearse drawn by two black horses came trundling round the back of the tavern; but, save for the undertaker and his bearer, not a soul appeared at the funeral. When they entered the shack where the body had lain they were startled to find an empty coffin. The corpse had vanished during the night, and Evan Du was never seen there again. The coffin, with no name inscribed upon it, was filled with stones and carried off many miles, there to be buried outside the churchyard walls.

CHAPTER 19

". . . Why don't you answer? . . ."

The night had passed slowly for John and Emma. From the room in the attic they had listened for further sounds of galloping hooves and the baying of the Hounds of Hell. But, with the Devil's errand fulfilled, all signs of his bearers had passed. During the hours of darkness they had heard only the voices of the revellers who had remained in the tavern.

As the night wore on, John had fallen asleep, leaving Emma to keep watch at his bedside, or to gaze from the window, longing for the silhouette of Poll to appear on the horizon. She did not think it strange that she shouldn't feel sleepy herself.

When dawn broke, the tavern had become quiet, for the Gwylnos was over and everyone had gone home. When the old women were back in their room the children had stolen away, fearful that Agatha or Jessie might wonder what spirits were abroad, and search the mysteries of their looking-glass.

"They never seem to sleep – nor even close their eyes!" John had said as they crept down the stairs, glancing furtively into every dark corner.

Now they were making their way along the path they had taken with Old Josiah. The sun was peeping over the hills,

161

and the grass was glistening silver with dew. Behind them, green footprints trailed across the hillside where John had trodden, but not a mark showed in Emma's wake. Looking back, they could see the darker green of the tavern walls smothered in their ivy coat, half-hidden among the trees. They were relieved to see the house getting smaller each time they paused to look around, and to find no one hurrying in pursuit.

Presently they sat on a dry-stone wall to rest. The tavern was now a mile or more away, but still their eyes scanned the horizon and were sometimes raised to the sky, afraid that two black crows would be hovering there.

"I believe the house has always been bewitched!" said Emma, reflecting on its transformation through summers past and time yet to come. "Perhaps it's like a ghost, appearing from nowhere and then fading away when its haunting is done."

John turned to her with some misgiving – to her misty figure which allowed the wall and the hills beyond to show through. "The house has stood there for more than a hundred years," he answered reproachfully. "It's you who appears from nowhere and often vanishes with the darkness! Who else but a ghost could pass through closed doors as easily as smoke drifts up the chimney?"

"Then shall I drift away and leave you all alone?" asked Emma, raising her voice.

"Please don't go! When you're away I have no one – not a friend in all the world!" John looked at her with his deep brown eyes.

Emma pondered for a while. "Perhaps I am the one who is real," she argued, "and Tŷ-yn-y-Cysgodion and all those I see there have come to haunt me. Why, only yesterday, when I returned, the tavern wasn't there at all!"

"But houses never simply vanish. It only seems so when they are hidden in the mist or the darkness."

"The place where it always stands was just a dell," Emma explained. "A clearing in the woods, where tall reeds grew and children were playing around a magic pool – still and clear like a looking-glass."

"Maybe you'd lost your way? I sometimes do when I'm gathering kindling in the woods."

"Strange reflections appeared in the water," Emma went on. "I saw a dense forest which rippled away when the wind stirred the surface. And when the water was calm again, the scene had changed. The trees were gone, leaving the hills and valley bare. It was as though time were rushing by, showing glimpses of the past!"

"*Dirgelaidd Dwr!*" whispered John. "Mysterious waters, or pools of magic. There are many tales of them."

"And once I saw the tavern reflected there, all black and fallen to ruin – a picture of some future time, perhaps. Not one of the children glanced my way, even when I drew close enough to stare into their faces. Instead, they ran to the edge of the woods where someone was calling to them."

Emma fell silent for a time, past incidents stirring in her memory. It seemed that the magic pool and the looking-glass hanging in the Devil Sisters' room held the same enchanted power, both reflecting pictures of different times and different places. She remembered the water, first shimmering and then still, with scenes of winter and summer swiftly passing, the children gathered around the pool calling to the spirit of *Dirgelaidd Dwr*.

Then she recalled Agatha and Jessie sprinkling herbs on the fire, the coloured flames and purple smoke billowing up the chimney. "*Dirgelaidd Dwr . . . Pwll Cyfareddol . . .*"

163

they had muttered in their spell.

"Somehow," said Emma thoughtfully, "the Devil Sisters have captured the magic of the enchanted pool and hidden it in their looking-glass. And if ever it were smashed the spell would be broken."

But now they knew that it would hang in the corner of their room until Tŷ-yn-y-Cysgodion fell to ruin.

"The spirit of the magic pool!" breathed John. "Perhaps that's what was calling to the children."

Emma shook her head. "No – not the voice of a spirit. Standing there under the trees were the Devil Sisters! And although time had changed the woods and hills, and the tavern walls were crumbled, they were the same as ever, with their tattered clothes and withered cheeks and voices like the cawing of crows!"

John looked about him as though he were expecting dark wings above them to spread shadows over the ground, and dared to hope that the mountain stream they had crossed would keep the witches at bay.

"So you see," Emma concluded, "maybe Tŷ-yn-y-Cysgodion is just a vision, and only ghosts visit there. It's all so bewildering!"

John was puzzled, too – not knowing what to believe. "If it's truly a vision, and everyone who stays there is part of it," he argued, "then I must be a ghost from long ago!" He began to laugh, for the possibility of *his* being a ghost seemed too preposterous for anyone to accept. "And that night you told me of – that night at the fair, where you listened to a fortune-teller and came upon a preacher in the crowd – it must have been the ghost of Old Josiah's *ghost* you saw!"

Then Emma smiled, too, trying hard to unravel the mystery of it all.

Looking back along the path they had taken, John could see that the tavern had not vanished nor fallen to ruin. It was still standing among the trees, a grim reminder of his long days of misery and loneliness there. "Don't go away for always, Emma," he pleaded, almost in tears. "If, by chance, you are a ghost, then promise that you will haunt me for ever."

As they rested there, they could hear the distant bleating of sheep and the song of an early skylark. And then, far off at first, but getting louder as it approached, they heard a sound that dispelled all thoughts of ghosts and enchanted waters. From over the shoulder of a hill came a chestnut mare, whinnying and tossing her head in excitement.

"It's Poll!" Emma cried; and they ran to meet her.

Her coat was glistening with sweat, and her eyes were bright, now more from fear than fury. She nuzzled into John's chest, pressing so hard that he staggered back, laughing at the warmth of her greeting. Emma fancied that she was remembered, too, for the mare held her head still and twitched her nostrils when she stretched out her hand and whispered: "Poor old girl. Were you afraid there was no one to care for you?"

As the sun rose higher, they proceeded on their journey, from high in the saddle looking ahead to the hills and dales smudged with heather; and once in a while turning to look back, until the woods and the tavern had fallen from sight below the horizon.

Perhaps it was the glare of the sun or the gentle motion of her swaying from side to side that caused Emma to close her eyes. Before long, however, there was darkness everywhere, and a rushing in her ears, as though slowly she were sinking and drifting along beneath the surface of the *Dirgelaidd Dwr* . . .

165

When Emma opened her eyes she could distinguish familiar shapes, black against the lesser darkness of her room. Downstairs, the clocks in her grandfather's curiosity shop were chiming the passing of the hour. There was no other sound. One! she counted; and wondered whether now she was alone. Two! It hadn't been a dream, for in dreams scenes swiftly fade and leave no lasting memory. Yet even now she could feel the rhythmic jogging of Poll's hooves along the paths, and see, in her mind, the hills folding in the distance. Three! Four! came the tolling of clocks. Then John must be riding on, unaware that she was no longer clinging on behind him. If only they had some magic pool of their own – some talisman like the Devil Sister's looking-glass with which they could see into the unknown. Then they would never be far apart.

The clocks did not strike again. It was four o'clock – an hour or more before the first light of dawn, and a longer time of listening and wondering before her grandparents stirred. The streets, the house, were wrapped in sleep – so quiet that Emma could hear her heart beating as she lay on her pillow. Memories of the Wake Night at the tavern came tumbling through her thoughts: the singing by candlelight, then the darkness and murmurs, followed by a wailing and the trample of hooves heralding the advance of the Devil's cortége, Agatha and Jessie huddled together, their shoulders rocking with laughter. No nightmare could have been so vivid.

Then her thoughts strayed to John, guiding Poll over the hills, not knowing where his journey would end, but travelling on and on, each step taking him farther from the House in the Shadows. In her picture of Tŷ-yn-y-Cysgodion lying in the cellar, never again would she see a light burning in the attic window.

Emma closed her eyes, and another hour passed. she woke again and opened her bedroom curtains t darkness was fading. The street was deserted, and not a wisp of smoke curled from the chimneys. She discovered that her grandfather had awakened early, too, for she heard him pottering around downstairs, long before it was time to open the shutters of the curiosity shop. Surprised at his early rising, she slipped on her dressing-gown and went to the top of the stairs. From there she saw no lamplight below, and wondered why he should be moving about in the near darkness.

"Grandad!" she called, at first in a whisper, not wishing to disturb her grandmother who was surely still asleep. But her voice was lost among the ticking of the clocks.

She could hear the old man's footsteps shuffling about: into the little room where usually he tinkered with his cogs and pendulums; then back to the shelves near the window, pausing there for a while before making his way to the corner of the shop where there was no light at all.

"Grandad!" she called again, a little louder and from half-way down the stairs. "What are you doing? It's not long past daybreak!"

No answer came from the room below, only the tick-ticking of the clocks, as fast as the beating of her heart.

"Grandad?" she called once more, quite distinctly now, not caring whether her grandmother was awake or asleep. In reply she heard old Mr Dalamore's footfalls descending to the cellar.

After waiting a while, she went down among the ticks and tocks and occasional chimes. And from the open doorway above the steps she listened to his rummaging among the broken pictures and curios that littered the cellar.

167

f the stairway her voice came echoing
e were calling into a cavern. "It's so dark
here. Shall I fetch a lamp . . . *lamp*?"
ice followed; and then: "Grandad, why
. . . *answer*?"

away when, at last, her grandfather was
heard climbing the steps. And a moment later his silhouette
appeared at the top.

"You'll find nothing down there in the dark!" said
Emma, walking ahead of him and picking her way around a
jumble of oddments strewn upon the floor. "Whatever
were you searching for?" she went on, turning to complain
at his wandering about in the early hours of the morning.

But the words were frozen on her lips. At first she could
only stare with fright. Then her screams echoed through
the house as she fled in terror up the stairs and along the
landing. For when the figure emerged from the darkness it
was not her grandfather she saw. The stranger was dressed
all in black, with a scarred face and fiery eyes. And his
arms were stretched out towards her!

CHAPTER 20

". . . Why do you tremble, my pretty? . . ."

Emma's screams woke her grandparents and brought them to the landing, startled by the sudden outcry. They pounded on the bedroom door while, from inside, Emma continued to cry out in terror. In the farthest corner of the room she hid, her eyes wide with fear.

A long time passed before she could be persuaded that it was not Evan Du who waited outside, trying to force his way in; and minutes more before she unlocked the door and fell crying into her grandmother's arms. Through sobs and tears she rambled on about some servant of the Devil who had come from long ago to seek her out.

Her grandmother held her close. "There's no one to harm you," she said. "It's over now. Your nightmares have gone."

Emma said no more. How were they ever to understand that the ghosts of Tŷ-yn-y-Cysgodion did not come to her in dreams, but beckoned her from far away, and sometimes followed when she returned from her journey there – just as the fortune-teller had foreseen? How could they believe that if only the secret paths were known, the past was no farther away than a moment measured on her grandfather's clocks?

As the day wore on and the sky brightened, Emma's

fears subsided. She tried to believe that it had after all been a nightmare, as her grandmother had said. But her fears were rekindled when darkness fell and the house was quiet again. There were occasions at this time of night or in the early hours of the morning when she fancied she heard the footsteps of someone moving up and down the stairs; but always she was too afraid to venture outside her bedroom door, or to tell anyone of the presence of an uninvited visitor.

"It's bad dreams that come to torment you," her grandmother kept repeating. "Your thoughts are always dwelling on stories from years gone by – on memories that are best forgotten."

Day after day she looked anxiously at her grand-daughter and rarely left her alone to brood and wonder.

One night Emma woke from her sleep and felt compelled to open her curtains and look down into the street. There, standing under the lamplight, she imagined she saw Evan Du staring up at her window. With a startled cry, she stepped back out of sight, but when she dared to look again he was gone.

And so the days went by, with Emma always wrapped in memories and day-dreams of faraway places and forgotten people.

Sometimes, before she went to sleep, her grandfather would sit on the bed beside her to keep her company – to ask what she had learned at school, or tell of his day in the curiosity shop and the customers who came in search of bargains.

But whenever she had a chance Emma would lead their conversation to the picture that lay in the cellar, or to recollections of what the fortune-teller had foreseen in her tarot cards and crystal ball. For it was the mysteries of time and the inhabitants of Tŷ-yn-y-Cysgodion that constantly filled her thoughts.

"Why does no one believe me?" she pleaded one evening while she and her grandfather were together. "Why does no one understand? Nightmares are never so real. They don't come time and time again, by night and day!"

For a while the old man sat there quietly. Then, with a smile, he said: "My Beautiful Dreamer. There are times when your imagination carries you away to some Never-Never Land, and that's a lonely place to be. Don't be sad. We shall always be with you."

Emma turned to look at him. "Never-Never Land?" she frowned.

"That far-off place we visit in our dreams," her grandfather explained. "And when you begin to wander there we're sometimes afraid you might never return. That's what worries us so."

Emma sat up beside him. It was comforting that someone should listen to her troubles – that someone should try to understand. "Wherever I go I shall always come back again," she said. "Don't you remember the fortune-teller's promise? 'However far you travel, you will always return.' It was written in the picture cards, and clear in her crystal ball."

The old man was smiling still, and Emma was encouraged to confide in him further. "'But sometimes,' the fortune-teller warned, 'the folk you meet on your journey will follow when you return.' You remember: 'Misty shapes – like ghosts coming to haunt you.' That's what she saw in my future. Evan Du has come to me from long ago!" she went on. "Yet it can't be me he's searching for. I was just a ghost in his time. I wonder . . ."

She pondered for a minute. It was becoming clear to her now. "It's the picture!" she whispered under her breath, remembering how once the painted trees and clouds had stirred, and the picture of the shadowy house hanging under the lamplight downstairs had beckoned her into the past. "Perhaps there is no other path to Tŷ-yn-y-Cysgodion. Perhaps it was only I who knew the way there. Now that Evan Du is dead and gone, his ghost is drifting about like a ship lost at sea, seeking the place and the time where he belongs."

Old Mr Dalamore brushed away a lock of hair that had fallen over his granddaughter's forehead. "Then now, at last, the ghost has found 'its' way. There'll be no more searching – no more wandering like that ship lost in the ocean. The ghost has gone forever. So you must forget your Never-Never Land, and stay here where *you* belong."

So saying, the old man stood up and stretched his aching back. "Just like the old rhyme your great-grandad used to recite when I was a boy," he added with a grin. "Sometimes at Hallowe'en he would turn down the lamp and drape mother's black shawl over his head and shoulders. Then we would hear a deep voice say:

> 'Yesterday, upon the stair,
>   I met a man who wasn't there.
> He wasn't there again today;
>   And how I wish he'd go away!'

"And then we would all laugh, and my sisters would hide under the table, even though we knew he was only teasing."

Emma, too, found herself longing that this 'man who wasn't there' had now gone away, never to be seen or heard again; for there was no one, save the Devil Sisters themselves, whom she feared more than he. She was still reflecting on his evil ways and the Devil's cortège which came after dark to carry him off when her grandfather closed the bedroom door behind him.

For hours Emma lay awake that night, listening for the sound of footsteps downstairs. At any moment she expected to hear someone climbing to the landing and come knocking on her bedroom door. The footsteps would continue until she plucked up enough courage to peep outside. There she would see a figure dressed all in black. The candle flame would tremble and its light fall upon the scarred face of Evan Du! Her blood would turn to ice when he came closer . . . closer . . .

But Emma heard no unusual sound that night – no footfalls; no knocking on her door. The ghost, she wanted to believe, had gazed into the picture, and found a path through the trees. Already, perhaps, Evan Du had gone back to Tŷ-yn-y-Cysgodion, and was searching for the treasure hidden in his seafarer's bag.

Emma began to imagine how fearful a place it would be now that John was far away. Time and again she wondered where he might be and whether she would ever see him again. Perhaps he was wandering among the hills of Caernarfon, where some gipsy band might give him shelter and adopt him as their own? But then, maybe the Devil Sisters had followed his travels in their enchanted looking-glass? She shuddered at the thought of his being captured and confined again to the room in the attic. With all her heart she wished that he was free forever.

She hardly dared close her eyes, afraid that when she opened them again she would find herself moving along a path through the woods at Coed-y-Celyn. In the distance she would hear the sound of voices coming from a tavern.

There would no longer be lamplight in the attic window. John would be gone. But the tavern door would be ajar; and as she approached . . . Now her eyelids were becoming heavier and beginning to close . . . as she approached, two old women would be waiting in the doorway.

Suddenly, Emma sat up in bed. She had always suspected that it was the picture that drew her away. It was the picture that threw time into confusion and lured her to Tŷ-yn-y-Cysgodion. "If it weren't for that picture," she whispered to herself, "then the Devil Sisters – even the ghost of Evan Du – would always be a hundred years in the past!"

She woke often during the night, only to find that the familiar shapes in her bedroom had not changed.

The dawn drew nearer; but Emma waited until after daybreak before she tiptoed down to the cellar. There she took one last, lingering look into the picture, and then carried it to her room where she set a match to it in the grate. At last her journeying would be over, and she could escape the clutches of Evan Du and the spells of the Devil Sisters.

At first it smouldered slowly, singeing the surrounding trees and the ivy that clung to the tavern walls. Then there was a sudden burst of flames, burning with an intensity that lit up the room. She was driven back from the fireplace, raising her arms to shield her face from the heat. There was a crackling and a spluttering as smoke billowed from the grate. It was as though the very woods at Coed-y-Celyn had been set alight. The smoke brought tears to her eyes; and the last sound she remembered was a roaring in the chimney . . .

It was twilight when Emma rubbed her eyes and blinked away the tears – not the evening of the day she had awakened to; but some evening in the past. She found herself in a place she dared hope had gone forever. The sky was darkening, and a red glow appeared on the horizon. At first she thought it was the sun setting behind Tŷ-yn-y-Cysgodion; but then it glowed more fiercely, and clouds of smoke drifted across the sky. Soon the house was engulfed in flames which spilled out through the windows and wrapped around the walls.

The nearer Emma drew to the fire the more furiously it blazed. She thought it strange that no one was to be seen fleeing from the tavern: no cries were heard from within. And all the while her eyes were raised towards the attic, now hidden behind the pall of smoke and flames.

"John!" she cried, and went on calling his name, even though she hoped he was many miles away. But only the crackling of burning timbers came from inside. There was no sound nor sign of a living soul.

For a long time she stayed there: until the flames had petered out, and all that remained were the charred walls – just like the ruin she had once seen reflected in the *Dirgelaidd Dwr* . . .

In Emma's world of long ago, time described no constant pattern; and although she had stayed from dusk till dark, barely a minute had passed when she returned. The picture frame was still smouldering in the grate, and wisps of smoke were curling up the chimney. In her heart she knew that she had journeyed there for the last time, for now only the blackened walls of Tŷ-yn-y-Cysgodion stood there at the fringe of the woods. And its likeness – the picture that had first beckoned her into the past – had burned to ashes.

The autumn passed and winter wore on. Emma dreamed no more of the Devil Sisters, nor of Evan Du. But there were times, usually in the stillness of night as the timbers creaked, when she imagined she heard his footsteps on the stairs. Then she would wrap the bedclothes close about her, and dream instead of a boy with eyes so deep and dark as *Pwll Cyfareddol,* and hair that fell in heavy locks to his forehead. She wondered if, as the fortune-teller had foreseen, he would some day follow her from far away and long ago. How she longed to see him again some day, for there was a place in her heart for the gipsy boy as tender as that she saved only for her grandparents. If he belonged to her own time, his friendship would bring more joy than she had ever known. Her school-days would be filled with fun and happiness. And during the long holidays they could wander together to the hills, far from the drab streets of town.

But now that could never be, she reflected sadly. Now that the path to her Otherworld was lost, they would always be separated by a hundred summers. Evan Du and the Devil Sisters were banished to the past. She would never see them again. But wouldn't John have gone forever, too?

In her sadness she dared to hope that one day they would meet by chance; that he would not have grown old with the years that had passed, but remain as young as she remembered him. If, by some mystery – some magic of the *Dirgelaidd Dwr* – the path to Tŷ-yn-y-Cysgodion had not crumbled like the ashes in the grate, then there would always be a bridge spanning the present time and long ago.

Emma shuddered. Then the Devil Sisters and their black-hearted tavern keeper might seek her out. Yet, if ever this were to happen, then with her fear would come the excitement that her gipsy boy could find her too.

Always she would look for him whenever the gipsies came to town. And if, by chance, she should wander among the hills, she would watch for a chestnut mare, harnessed to a caravan or grazing near some camp fire. Never would she abandon her search, even when she grew to a young lady and he to a handsome man.

And search she did, through spring and summer and many seasons more, until she had almost forgotten the fear and sadness of her past journeys to the House in the Shadows.

It was one evening in winter when some gipsy beggars came along the street. First they peered through the window, and then made so bold as to come inside to offer old Mr Dalamore some unusual curios they had found in their travels.

Two old women they were. One, with shoulders bent, shuffled along with the aid of a knobbly stick, all the while muttering to herself. Her hair hung straight, streaked with grey. And when her muttering was done, she pursed her lips in an expression of surly displeasure. The other was gaunt, with furtive eyes that darted all about, as though nothing escaped their compass.

While her grandfather rummaged through their sack, examining the candlesticks and strings of beads and charm-stones gathered from the mountain streams, Emma could only stare in wonder, her cheeks as pale as death.

The two old women moved closer, stretching out their fingers to touch her hair.

"Well, now, who have we here?" the crooked one said in a husky voice. "Look, sister: a fair maid, with locks of new-spun gold and eyes as blue as the sky!"

"Why do you tremble, my pretty?" the gaunt one smiled.

177

She peered beyond the lamplight. "Is there a ghost hiding in the shadows?"

Postscript

House in the Shadows is a fictional story, interwoven with tales of folk belief prevalent long ago: tales gathered from the archives and from the old folk of Clwyd and Gwynedd.

As is mentioned in the first chapter, no one knows for sure where the tavern was situated. Some say that it stood on the fringe of the woodland at Coed-y-Celyn; others recall that it was near Pentre-foelas, on the border between Gwynedd and Glwyd. But it is generally agreed that somewhere along the fifteen-mile stretch from Cerrig-drudion and Betws-y-Coed, at a time when the A5 was just a rough road for horse and carriage, Tŷ-yn-y-Cysgodion (House in the Shadows) stood hidden among the trees.

Travellers on their way from England to Ireland sometimes broke their journey there, for a mug of ale and a night's rest. It is said that many of those who journeyed alone never reached their destination, but were robbed and murdered as they slept, their bodies concealed in shallow graves in the woods or buried beneath the flagstones in the cellar.

As rumours spread, and its evil reputation grew, Tŷ-yn-y-Cysgodion became deserted and eventually fell to ruin. Some say it was struck by lightning and burned until only its charred walls remained.

Prevalent too, in those long-gone days, were tales of *Dirgelaidd Dwr* (mysterious waters), of *Pwll Cyfareddoll* (pools or wells of magic), and of accounts of witchcraft.

Another mystery woven into the plot depicts the story recalled by an old lady who, as a girl, lived with her grandparents in a curiosity shop. It tells of an old painting stored in the cellar which so fascinated her that she became inexorably entangled in a world of fantasy.

These tales of folk belief, blended with fictitious characters and incidents form the skeleton of the foregoing story.